Dead Men Tell No Tales
and Other Stories

Émile Zola

Translated by Douglas Parmée

ALMA CLASSICS
an imprint of

ALMA BOOKS LTD
3 Castle Yard
Richmond
Surrey TW10 6TF
United Kingdom
www.almaclassics.com

The stories in this collection first published by Oxford University Press in the volume *The Attack on the Mill and Other Stories* in 1969
A revised version of these stories first published by Alma Classics in 2009 in the volume *Dead Men Tell No Tales*
Dead Men Tell No Tales and Other Stories first published by Alma Classics in 2017
English Translation © Douglas Parmée, 1969, 2009, 2017
Extra material © Larry Duffy, 2008

Printed in the United Kingdom by CPI Group (UK) Ltd, Croydon CR0 4YY

ISBN: 978-1-84749-696-6

Contents

Chronology

1840   Émile Zola born on 2nd April, in Paris, of French mother and Italian father.

1843   Family settles in Aix-en-Provence.

1847   Émile's father dies.

1859   Zola twice fails school-leaving *baccalauréat*.

1861   Destitute in Paris. Zola obtains post in shop of newly-founded firm of Hachette. Already writing poetry and short stories.

1864   In charge of Hachette's publicity. Publishes first collection of short stories, *Contes à Ninon*.

1865   Publication of first novel, *La Confession de Claude*. Liaison with Gabrielle-Alexandrine Meley; leaves Hachette, and embarks on writing career, at first largely as a journalist (reviewer, critic, short story and feature article writer).

1867   Favourable article on Manet's painting. As friend of Cézanne, frequents artistic circles, including many Impressionists. Publication of *Thérèse Raquin*.

1870   Marries Mlle Meley. Publication in serial form of *La Fortune des Rougon*, which becomes the first of the twenty-volume cycle of novels concerning the Rougon-Macquart family, published over the next twenty-three years. Takes refuge in Marseilles to avoid invading Prussian army; later becomes Parliamentary correspondent to French government, which had retreated to Bordeaux.

1871   Returns briefly to Paris but leaves to avoid Commune uprising.

1874   Publication of *Nouveaux contes à Ninon*.

1875   Beginning of collaboration with St Petersburg periodical *Vestnik Evropy* (*European Messenger*). Holiday in Saint-Aubin, on Normandy coast.

1876   Holiday in Piriac (see note to 'Shellfish for Monsieur Chabre').

1877   Success of *L'Assommoir*, seventh volume of *Rougon-Macquart* series, brings fame and financial security. Holiday in L'Estaque.

1878   Buys property in Médan, village on outskirts of Paris.

1880 Publication of *Soirées de Médan*. End of collaboration with *Vestnik Evropy*.

1882 Publication in France in one volume of six of Zola's *Vestnik Evropy* stories, under collective title of *Le Capitaine Burle*.

1883 Publication in one volume of further six of Zola's *Vestnik Evropy* stories, under collective title of *Naïs Micoulin*.

1885 Publication of *Germinal*, twelfth in the *Rougon-Macquart* series.

1888 Starts lifelong liaison with Jeanne Rozerot.

1889 Birth of Denise, daughter of Jeanne and Zola.

1891 Birth of Jacques, son of Jeanne and Zola.

1893 *Le Docteur Pascal* ends *Rougon-Macquart* series.

1894 Extended trip to Italy.

1898 Publication of Zola's article *J'Accuse* in Paris newspaper in favour of Dreyfus leads him to take refuge in England to avoid imprisonment. Writes his last story, 'The Haunted House' (*Angeline*).

1902 Death of Zola by asphyxiation in his Paris flat; suspicion that his bedroom chimney may have been deliberately blocked.

*Dead Men Tell No Tales
and Other Stories*

Captain Burle[*]

1

I T WAS NINE O'CLOCK and the inhabitants of Vauchamp had just gone to bed, leaving the little town in silence and darkness in the icy November rain. In the Rue des Récollets, one of the narrowest and most deserted in the St Jean district, just one lighted window remained on the third floor of an old house whose broken gutters were disgorging torrents of water. Madame Burle was still awake and sitting beside her meagre fire of vine stumps while her grandson Charles was doing his homework in the dim light of a lamp.

The flat which she rented for one hundred and twenty francs a year consisted of four enormous rooms, quite impossible to heat in winter. Madame Burle slept in the largest of them; her son, the regimental paymaster Captain Charles Burle, occupied the bedroom overlooking the street next to the dining room, and young Charles slept in an iron bedstead tucked away at the far end of the immense disused drawing room with its peeling wallpaper. The few sticks of furniture belonging to the captain and his mother, a solid mahogany Empire suite, dented and battered by many moves from one garrison town to another, were barely visible in the dim light which fell like a fine haze from the lofty ceiling. The cold, hard, red-painted floor tiles were freezing to the feet, for there were only a few odd squares of carpet in front of the chairs in this icy room swept by piercing draughts from the warped doors and window frames.

Madame Burle sat sunk in her yellow velvet armchair beside the fireplace, her face cradled in her hands, looking at the final wisps of smoke from a vine root with the vacant stare of an old woman living in the past. She would spend whole days sitting like this, a tall, long-faced figure whose thin lips never smiled. As the widow of a colonel who had died just as he was about to be made a general, and the mother of a captain, whom she had accompanied even throughout his campaigns, she had become imbued with ideas of duty, honour and patriotism

3

which had turned her into an unbending old lady, as it were shrivelled up by the harshness of strict military discipline. She rarely complained. When her son had been widowed after five years of marriage, she had undertaken her grandson's upbringing as a matter of course, like a sergeant sternly drilling his recruits. She ruled the child with a rod of iron, never tolerating the slightest caprice or unruly behaviour, making him work well into the night and staying up herself until midnight to see that his homework was completed. Under this harsh regime, Charles, who was a delicate, gentle little boy, was growing up pale and wan; he had fine eyes but they always seemed unnaturally bright and large.

One single thought was always turning over in Madame Burle's mind during her long periods of silent meditation: her son had let her down. She was obsessed by this idea and she would continually go back in her mind over her life, from the time of his birth, when she had seen him as a future hero who would reach the highest rank, in a blaze of glory, to the present narrow garrison life filled with the same dull, never-ending routine, his decline into the post of a regimental paymaster captain, from which he would never escape and in which he was becoming inert and apathetic. And yet there had been a time, at the beginning, when she had been proud of him: for a while she had been able to think that her dream was coming true. Burle had come straight out of the crack cavalry school of Saint-Cyr to distinguish himself by his gallantry at the battle of Solferino,* capturing a whole enemy battery with a handful of men. He was decorated, his heroism was reported in the papers and he became known as one of the bravest men in the army. Then slowly this hero had put on weight and become submerged in fat – relaxed, contented, stout, and cowardly. By 1870, he had not gone beyond the rank of captain. He was captured in his first skirmish and had returned from Germany an angry man, swearing that they wouldn't catch him fighting again, it was all too stupid. Being incapable of learning any other trade and so obliged to stay in the army, he had managed to obtain a post as regimental paymaster, a niche, he said, where at least they'd let him kick the bucket in peace. On the day this happened, Madame Burle had felt her heart break. Her dream had come to an end. Since then she had gritted her teeth and retreated implacably into her shell.

The wind was gusting down the Rue des Récollets and the windows shuddered under the deluge of rain. The old woman looked up from the dying embers of the vine stocks to make sure that Charles was not falling asleep over his Latin translation. This little lad of twelve had become her last hope of finally achieving her dogged ambition of making the name of Burle famous. At first she had loathed her grandson with all the hatred she had felt for his mother, a little lace-worker, pretty and delicate, whom the captain foolishly married when she had resisted his frantic attempts to make her his mistress. When his mother had died and his father had relapsed into a life of debauchery, Madame Burle had pinned all her hopes on her poor, sickly little grandson whom she was bringing up in such difficult circumstances. She wanted him to be strong, for he was to become the hero which Burle had failed to be, and so, in her cold, harsh way, she anxiously watched over him as he grew up, drumming courage into his head and feeling his limbs to test their strength. Little by little, blinded by her passionate ambition, she had come to believe that here at last was the man of the family. In fact, the child had a dreamy, tender nature and felt a physical horror of army life, but, being a very quiet, obedient boy and terrified of his grandmother, he repeated everything he was told and seemed resigned to becoming a soldier.

Meanwhile Madame Burle had noticed that the translation was not progressing very well. Bemused by the sound of the storm, Charles had dropped off to sleep, pen in hand, with his eyes still fixed on the paper. Her bony finger rapped sharply on the edge of the table and with a start he began feverishly thumbing the pages of his dictionary. Still without a word, the old woman began pulling the vine-stocks together in a vain attempt to rekindle the blaze.

During the period when she had still believed in her son, she had sacrificed all her savings and he had frittered away her meagre income in riotous living, the nature of which she had never dared investigate closely. Even now, he was ransacking the house and letting everything go to rack and ruin: they were on the brink of destitution, the rooms were stripped of furniture and hot meals a rare luxury. She never mentioned such things to him: with her respect for discipline, he still remained the master, the head of the house. Only sometimes she would shudder at the thought that Burle might well, one day, do something foolish that would prevent Charles from getting into the army.

As she stood up to fetch another vine branch from the kitchen, a terrible squall hit the house, rattling the doors, wrenching off a shutter and spilling a torrent of water from the broken gutters down onto the windows. Above the din, she was surprised to hear the doorbell ringing. Who could it be, at such a time and in such weather? Burle never came home before midnight, if indeed he came home at all. She opened up and an officer came in, soaked to the skin and swearing:

"Christ Almighty! What a foul night!"

It was the regimental adjutant Laguitte, a game old soldier who had served under Colonel Burle in the good old days. Born and bred in the barracks, he had risen, far more through courage than through intelligence, to the rank of battalion commander, when, as the result of a wound, a muscle contraction in his thigh had made him unfit for active service and forced him to accept a post as adjutant. He even had a slight limp, though you had to be careful not to tell him so to his face, because he refused to admit the idea.

"It's you, Major Laguitte," exclaimed Madame Burle in surprise.

"Yes, blast it!" growled Laguitte. "And I must be a damned fool and damned fond of you to be out in this damned rain... It's not fit weather to send a priest out in!"

He shook himself and his boots spread large puddles of water all over the floor. He looked around.

"I absolutely must see Burle! Is he in bed already, the lazy hound?"

"No, he's not home yet," the old woman replied in her gruff voice.

Laguitte looked exasperated.

"What? Not come home?" he exclaimed angrily. "In that case, they were having me on at that café of his, Mélanie's, you know all about it, don't you? I go in and there's this maid who laughs in my face and tells me that the captain's gone off to bed. Damn and blast it, I guessed as much, I was itching to tug her ears!"

He calmed down and walked round the room, looking upset and in two minds as to what to say next. Madame Burle was watching him closely.

"Did you want to speak to him personally?" she asked eventually.

"Yes," he replied.

"And I can't pass on a message for you?"

"No."

She did not insist but she still stood watching the adjutant who seemed unable to decide whether to leave or not. Finally, he burst out again:

"Ah well, can't be helped, damn and blast it! Since I'm here, you might as well know the truth, it'll probably be better."

And he sat down in front of the fireplace and stretched out his muddy boots as if there had been a bright fire blazing there. Madame Burle was just going back to her seat in the armchair when she noticed that, overcome by sleep, Charles's head had dropped onto the open pages of his dictionary. The adjutant's arrival had momentarily aroused him and then, seeing that no one was paying any attention, he had been unable to resist dropping off to sleep again. His grandmother was on her way to give him a rap on his hands, all white and frail in the light of the lamp, when Laguitte stopped her:

"Please don't, let the little fellow sleep. It's not very funny, he doesn't need to hear it."

The old woman went back to her armchair. Silence fell. They both looked at each other.

"Well, here goes," said the adjutant at last, emphasizing his remark with a vicious jerk of his chin, "this time that swine Burle has really done it!"

Madame Burle did not flinch, although her face grew pale as she sat up rigidly in her chair. The adjutant went on:

"I'd been suspecting something all along. I'd made up my mind to tell you about it one day. Burle was spending too much and he had an idiotic look on his face that worried me. But I never thought... Damn and blast it! How stupid can you get to play a dirty trick like that?"

He slapped his knee furiously again and again, speechless with indignation.

"He's been stealing?"

"You can't imagine what it is... Just think... I never used to check, myself, I passed all his accounts through. I merely signed at the bottom of the page. You know what it's like in the mess. Only when the annual inspection was coming up, because of the colonel, who's a bit of a stickler, I used to say: 'Watch your figures, old man, it's me who's got to carry the can!' And I didn't worry at all... All the same, for the last month or so, because he'd got such a queer look and people were saying some rather nasty things, I began looking a bit more closely into his accounts and going through his books. Everything seemed perfectly in order to me, nothing wrong at all..."

He broke off, seized by such a burst of rage that he had to let off steam straight away.

"Damn and blast it! It's not the swindling that annoys me, it's the beastly way he's behaved towards me! He's made a bloody fool of me. Madame Burle, do you realize?... Blast him! Does he think I'm an old idiot?"

"So he's been stealing?" his mother asked again.

"This evening," the adjutant went on, somewhat more calmly, "I'd just finished dinner when in comes Gagneux. You know Gagneux, the butcher on the corner of the Place aux Herbes. And there's another damned scoundrel, too, who got the contract and then feeds our men on old cows' meat from God knows where! So I greet him like the dirty dog he is and he proceeds to take the lid off the whole rotten business. And what a business! Apparently Burle only ever gave him payment on account, a real swindle, and such an unholy muddle that it'll be the devil's own job to straighten it out. To cut a long story short, Burle owes him two thousand francs and the butcher is talking of going to spill the beans to the colonel if he doesn't get his money... But the worst thing of all is that that swine Burle, to land me in the soup, used to give me a false receipt every week which he simply signed in Gagneux's name. Fancy playing a trick like that on an old friend like me! Damn and blast the whole bloody thing!"

Laguitte stood up waving his fists in the air and then fell back again in his chair.

"So he's been stealing," Madame Burle said again. "It was bound to happen."

Then, without a word of judgement or condemnation of her son, she added simply:

"We haven't got two thousand francs. We might have thirty francs in the house."

"I suspected that," said Laguitte. "And do you know where all the money goes? It goes to Mélanie, a trollop who's driven Burle crazy... Women! I said before that they'd be the ruination of him! I just don't know what's wrong with that swine. He's only five years younger than me and he still can't keep away from them, the randy old goat!"

There was another silence. Outside the rain was pouring down harder than ever and in the sleeping little town you could hear the crash of slates and chimney pots brought down by the gale.

"Ah well," said the adjutant, getting to his feet, "we shan't settle anything by sitting here talking... It was just to warn you. I must be off."

"What can we do?" asked the old woman in a low voice. "Is there anyone we can approach?"

"Don't be downhearted, we'll just have to see. If only I had two thousand francs of my own... But I've no money, as you know."

He stopped short in embarrassment. He was an old bachelor, with no wife or children, and he systematically drank all his pay, and anything left over from his bills for absinthe* and brandy he lost at gambling. With all that, a very honest man, on principle.

"Never mind," he went on, standing in the doorway, "I'll still go along and rout out the old rascal at his lady-love's. I'll move heaven and earth... Burle, the son of *the* Burle, condemned for theft! It'd be the end of the world, it can't be possible! I'd sooner blow the whole place up... So don't worry, confound it all! It's even more annoying for me!"

He gripped her hand tightly and disappeared into the shadow of the staircase while she held up the lamp to light his way. When she had put the lamp down on the table, she stood motionless for a moment in the enormous bare and silent room and a flush of tenderness rose to her cheeks as she looked pensively at Charles, still asleep with his face resting on the pages of his dictionary: with his long fair hair and pale complexion he looked like a little girl. But this tenderness which softened her harsh, cold features lasted only a second before her face set once more into its usual air of grim determination. Sharply, she rapped the boy's hand:

"Your translation, Charles!"

The lad woke up with a shiver and with a scared look began hurriedly turning over the pages of his dictionary. At that very moment Laguitte, slamming the street door behind him, was drenched from head to foot with a downpour of rain from the gutter and his swearing could be heard even above the storm. Then the only sound audible against the pounding rain was the gentle scratch of Charles's pen on the paper. Madame Burle had gone back to her seat in front of the fireplace and was sitting as she always sat every evening, as stiff as a ramrod, staring at the dead embers of the fire, lost in her dogged obsession.

2

THE CAFÉ DE PARIS, kept by the widow Madame Mélanie Cartier, stood in the Place du Palais, a large irregular square planted with dusty oaks. In Vauchamp people would say: "Coming to Mélanie's?" Here, at the end of the first room, quite a large one, there was a second room, called the "sofa room", which was very narrow, with imitation leather upholstered sofas running all round the walls and four marble tables standing in the corners, and it was here that Mélanie, leaving the bar in the charge of her maid Phrosyne, would spend her evenings in the company of a few "regulars", an inner circle who were known in the town as the "sofa-room gentlemen". It was a hallmark: thereafter, every mention of their names would evoke smiles in which condemnation competed with secret envy.

Madame Cartier had been widowed at the age of twenty-five. Her husband had been a wheelwright who had astounded Vauchamp by taking over the Café de Paris on the death of an uncle, and one fine morning he had brought her back from Montpellier, which he visited every six months to lay in his supply of liqueurs. As part of the equipment of setting up his business, he had taken a wife, doubtless to his taste, who was prepossessing and likely to increase the consumption of alcohol. No one ever discovered where he'd picked her up, and indeed he didn't actually marry her until after a six months' trial period behind the bar. As a matter of fact, opinions on Mélanie were divided: some said she was superb; others described her as bossy. She was tall, with pronounced features and coarse hair which came right down to her eyebrows. But nobody denied her ability to twist men round her little finger. She had fine eyes and she used them shamelessly to gaze at her "sofa-room gents" until they grew pale and amenable. And rumour had it also that she was a fine figure of a woman: in the Midi, that's the sort of woman they like...

Cartier had died in a strange way. There was talk of a squabble between the couple and of an abscess brought about by a kick in the stomach. However that might be, Mélanie found herself very awkwardly placed, for the café was not doing at all well. The wheelwright had squandered his uncle's money by drinking his own absinthe and spending lengthy sessions at his own billiard table. For a while it looked as though she would have to sell up. But she liked the life and for a lady, everything was laid on. She never needed more than a few customers and the front room could remain empty. So all she did was to put white and gold paper on the walls and new imitation leather on the sofas. First of all she entertained a pharmacist in her newly decorated room; there followed a spaghetti manufacturer, a solicitor and a retired magistrate. And by these means the café remained open, although the waiter hardly served twenty drinks a day. The authorities turned a blind eye as long as the proprieties were observed; after all, a lot of respectable people would have been compromised.

In the evening, half a dozen locals, men with modest private means, would still come in for their game of dominoes in the big front room: Cartier was dead and some queer goings-on were taking place in the Café de Paris but they saw nothing and kept to their old habits. As the waiter was proving superfluous, Mélanie got rid of him and now it was Phrosyne who would light the single gaslight in the corner for their game. Occasionally, attracted by the stories they had heard and egging each other on "to go to Mélanie's", a gang of young men would burst into the bar room, laughing loudly to hide their embarrassment. They would be greeted with icy dignity; they rarely saw the proprietress or, if she happened to be there, she overwhelmed them with her beauty and her disdain, leaving them completely at a loss for words. She was far too intelligent to forget herself and behave in any way foolishly. While the main room remained in darkness, lit only in the corner where the gentlemen of leisure were performing their ritual game of dominoes, she would serve the sofa-room regulars herself: friendly but discreet, she would occasionally give way to an impulse, if she felt so inclined, to rest her arm on the shoulder of one of them to follow some particularly neat play in their game of écarté.

One evening these gentlemen, who had grown to tolerate each other's presence, were disagreeably surprised to discover Captain Burle ensconced on one of the sofas. He had, it seemed, come in that morning, quite by chance, to have a glass of vermouth. Mélanie was alone and they had chatted together. That evening, when he came back, Phrosyne had shown him straight away into the small back room.

Two days later, Burle was the reigning monarch, without, however, putting the pharmacist, the spaghetti manufacturer, the solicitor or the retired magistrate to flight. The captain, a short, broad man, adored tall women. In the regiment he was nicknamed Skirty because of his constant womanizing, a taste he satisfied whenever and however he could and all the more vigorously when there was an extra large morsel to enjoy. Whenever the officers or even the ordinary soldiers saw some great bag of flesh with incredibly opulent charms, a veritable giant balloon of fat, whether she was dressed in fine clothes or in rags, they would exclaim: "Just the job for Skirty!" Everything was grist to his mill and in the barrack room of an evening, they all prophesied that it would be the death of him. And so that "fine figure of a woman" took him completely and irresistibly into her power; he sank without trace into her capacious maw. It took him no longer than a fortnight to be reduced to an amorous stupor, a fat little man drained dry, even though he was still as fat as ever. His tiny eyes lost in his bloated face would follow her everywhere she went, like the eyes of a beaten dog, and the sight of that broad masculine face with its coarse bristly hair held him in a constant ecstasy of delight: he could think of nothing else. For fear that she might stop his rations, as he put it, he was prepared to tolerate the presence of the "sofa-room gentlemen" and forked out the last farthing of his pay. The situation was summed up by a sergeant: "Skirty has found his hole and he'll not budge." A man as good as dead!

It was nearly ten o'clock when Major Laguitte flung open the door of the Café de Paris. Through the doorway, as the door slammed behind him, you could catch a glimpse of the Place du Palais, pitch-dark and like a mud lake bubbling under the pouring rain. Wet to the skin by now and leaving a trail of water behind him, the adjutant made straight for the bar where Phrosyne was sitting reading a novel. "So that's the way you make a fool of an officer, you bitch!" he shouted. "I ought to…"

And he swung his arm as though to give her a box on the ears that would have sent her flying. The frightened little maid shrank back while the domino players turned round to look, open-mouthed, unable to understand what it was all about. But the adjutant wasted no time; he pushed open the sofa-room door and went in at the very moment that Mélanie was charitably engaged in offering the captain his grog in tiny spoonfuls, like a pet canary. That evening the only other customers had been the retired magistrate and the pharmacist and they had both left early, in a depressed mood. And as Mélanie needed three hundred francs the following day, she was seizing the opportunity of wheedling them out of the captain.

"Come along luvvy duvvy... Give Mummy your little beaky-weaky... It's good, isn't it, you naughty little boy..."

Flabby and goggle-eyed, the captain, purple in the face, was sucking the spoon in a paroxysm of pleasure.

"Christ Almighty!" bellowed the adjutant standing in the doorway. "You're getting women to look after you now, are you? They told me you hadn't come and told me to go away and all the time you're here going barmy!"

Burle sat up and pushed the grog away. Mélanie stepped forwards, looking annoyed, as if she wanted to protect him with her large frame. But Laguitte looked her squarely in the eyes with that determined expression that is very familiar to women running the risk of getting their face slapped.

"Get out!" he said simply.

She still hesitated for a second but when she could almost hear the slap whistling past her ear, white with rage she went out to join Phrosyne at the bar.

When they were alone at last, Laguitte took up his stance in front of the captain and then, crossing his arms, he bent forwards and with all his might yelled:

"You dirty bastard!"

Completely taken aback, the other man was on the point of losing his temper but Laguitte did not give him time.

"Shut up! What a dirty trick to play on a friend... You plastered me with dud receipts which could have landed both of us in jail. Is that a decent thing to do? How could you play that sort of dirty game when we've known each other for thirty years?"

Burle subsided into his seat and went ghastly pale. He was trembling feverishly all over. Walking round him and banging his fist on the table, the major went on:

"So you've turned into a miserable little petty thief of a clerk, have you? And all for that cow out there, too!... If you'd done it for your mother, that would at least have been something honourable but cooking the accounts and then bringing the proceeds round to this lousy place, that's what makes me sick, for Christ's sake!... Well? What the hell's gone wrong with your head to knock yourself up at your age with a bossy old sow like that? Don't give me any blarney, I saw the pair of you playing your little games a moment ago!"

13

"You go gambling yourself," faltered the captain.

"Yes, I do, damn you," the adjutant replied, even more infuriated by this remark, "and I'm a damned fool to do it because I'm losing every penny I've got and it's no credit to the French army. But Christ Almighty, if I do gamble, I don't go in for stealing! Kill yourself if you like and let your mother and your little lad starve but at least keep your fingers out of the till and don't land your friends in the shit!"

He stopped. Burle sat staring with an idiotic look on his face. For a second, the only sound to be heard was the clumping of the major's boots.

"And not a bean!" he went on violently. "Well? Can you see yourself with the handcuffs on? Oh, you rotten bastard!"

He calmed down, seized Burle by the wrist and dragged him to his feet.

"Come along! We've got to do something at once, I shan't get a wink of sleep with this on my mind... I've got an idea."

In the large front bar, Mélanie and her maid were excitedly whispering to each other. When Mélanie saw the two men emerge, she was bold enough to go up to them and say, in her most ingratiating voice: "What's the matter, captain? Are you off so soon?"

"Yes, he is," Laguitte replied curtly, "and I don't expect him ever to set foot in your dirty hole again."

The little maid caught her mistress by the arm and was unwise enough to mutter the word "drunk", whereupon the adjutant finally let fly with the slap that he'd been itching to give for some time. The two women ducked and he succeeded only in hitting the back of Phrosyne's neck, flattening her bonnet and breaking her comb. The gentlemen of independent means were indignant.

"Hell, let's go," said Laguitte, pushing Burle out on to the pavement. "If I stay, I'll bash the lot of them in there."

As they crossed the square the water came up to their ankles. The wind drove the rain streaming down their faces. As they walked along, the captain said nothing when the adjutant started once more to tell him off, even more angrily than before, for his "fart-arsing about". "Lovely weather for a walk, wasn't it? If he hadn't been so stupid, they'd both be snug in bed instead of paddling about like this." He went on to talk about Gagneux. A complete and utter rogue whose rotten meat had given the whole regiment the squitters three times already. His contract expired next week. The devil if they'd accept his tender for the next one!

"That's my pigeon, I can choose who I like," grunted the adjutant. "I'd sooner lose my right arm than let that poisoner get another penny out of us!"

He swore profusely as he slipped up to his knees in a gutter and then said:

"I'm going to see him... You wait outside while I go up... I want to find out if he's really got the guts to go and see the colonel tomorrow, as he was threatening to do... A butcher, for Christ's sake! Fancy getting involved with a butcher! God, you're certainly not proud. That's one thing I'll never forgive you for."

They had reached the Place aux Herbes. Gagneux's house was in darkness but Laguitte knocked vigorously on the door and it was eventually opened. Left alone in the dark, Captain Burle did not even think of seeking shelter but stood motionless in the pouring rain at the corner of the market square. His head was buzzing and he felt quite incapable of thought. He did not feel bored, for he had lost all sense of time. With its windows and doors all closed, the house seemed dead; he just stood looking at it. When the adjutant emerged an hour later, it seemed to Burle as if he had only just gone in.

Laguitte looked sombre and said nothing. The captain did not dare ask any questions. For a brief moment they looked for each other, dimly, in the gloom. Then they set off once again through the dark streets that were like some river bed in spate. They groped their way along side by side, in silence. Absorbed in his thoughts, Laguitte had even stopped cursing. However, when they were once again crossing the Place du Palais, seeing that the Café de Paris was still lit up, he tapped Burle on the shoulder and said:

"If you ever go back to that hole again..."

"Don't worry," the captain replied, not letting him finish his sentence. And he held out his hand. But Laguitte went on:

"No, I'll take you as far as your house, so that I can at least be sure you won't go back there again tonight."

They walked on. As they went down the Rue des Récollets, they both slackened their pace. Then, having reached his door, the captain took his keys out of his pocket and at last decided to speak:

"Well?" he asked.

"Well," replied the adjutant gruffly, "I'm as big a bastard as you... I've played a shit's trick... God blast your eyes! Our men are going to have to eat rotten meat for another three months."

And he explained that Gagneux, as well as being a disgusting little man, was a crafty bugger who had gradually led him on to make a deal: he wouldn't go and see the colonel, he'd even forget about the two thousand francs and give Laguitte properly signed receipts in exchange for the false ones, but in return he insisted that his tender would be accepted for the next allocation of supplies of meat to the regiment. It was a bargain.

"So you see," Laguitte went on, "just think what a packet he must be making in order to be able to let us off those two thousand francs!"

Choking with emotion, Burle gripped his old friend's hands, unable to do more than stammer a few confused words of thanks and moved to tears at the thought that the adjutant had just perpetrated such a dishonest action purely in order to save him.

"It's the first time I've ever done a thing like that," grunted the adjutant, "but it was the only way... Damn and blast it! Fancy not having two thousand francs tucked away in one's drawer! It's enough to put you off gambling for good... Well, it's my bad luck! I'm a pretty poor sort of chap... Anyway, just listen to me: don't do it again, because I certainly won't, for Christ's sake!"

The captain gave him a hug and when he had gone in, the adjutant stood for a moment by the door to make sure he had gone to bed. Then, as it was striking midnight and the rain was still pelting down, he made his way laboriously home through the streets now plunged in darkness, sick at heart at the thought of what he had done to his men. He stopped and said out loud in a changed voice, full of affection and pity:

"Poor buggers! Think of all the old cow they'll be eating for the sake of two thousand francs!"

3

THE REGIMENT WAS STUPEFIED. Skirty had broken off with Mélanie. By the end of the week, there was proof positive: the captain was no longer setting foot in the Café de Paris; it was being said that the pharmacist had slipped into his place, almost before it was cold, to the great chagrin of the former magistrate. And, even more incredibly, Captain Burle was now cloistered in the Rue des Récollets. He was definitely settling down, to the point of spending all his evenings at his own fireside, going over Charles's lessons with him. His mother, who had never breathed a word to him about his unsavoury dealings with Gagneux, sat in her armchair as before, looking as strict and stern as ever, but in her eyes you could read the belief that he was cured.

One evening, a fortnight later, Laguitte decided to invite himself to dinner. He felt some embarrassment at the thought of seeing Burle again, not, indeed, on his own account but on the captain's, fearing that it might bring back painful memories. However, since the captain was a reformed character, he made up his mind to call on him and have a spot of dinner together.

When Laguitte arrived, the captain was in his room and it was Madame Burle who let him in. After announcing that he had come to take pot luck, he enquired in a whisper:

"Well?"

"Everything's all right," replied the old lady.

"Nothing fishy?"

"Absolutely nothing... In bed by nine o'clock, not a single late night, and he seems very cheerful."

"Well I'm damned! That's wonderful!" exclaimed the adjutant. "I knew he needed a good shake-up. His heart's still in the right place, the old devil!"

When Burle appeared, he gave him a hearty handshake and before sitting down to dinner, they stayed chatting genially in front of the fire, singing the praises of domesticity. The captain declared that he wouldn't change his home for a king's ransom; when he'd taken off his braces, put on his slippers and stretched out in his armchair, he wouldn't call the king his cousin, he said. The adjutant agreed as he eyed him closely. It was certainly true that his change of heart had not made him any thinner; in fact, he seemed to have swollen as, with goggle-eyes and puffy lips, he sat half asleep slumped in his chair, saying again and again:

"There's nothing like family life! Family life's the thing for me!"

"That's splendid," said the adjutant, worried at seeing him looking so completely exhausted, "but don't overdo it, will you?... Take some exercise, go to a café now and again."

"What would I be doing in a café... I've got everything I want here. No, I'm staying at home."

Charles was tidying away his books when Laguitte was surprised to see a maid come in to lay the table.

"You've taken someone on?" he said.

"We had to," Madame Burle replied with a sigh. "My legs aren't much good these days and everything was getting neglected... Luckily old Cabrol let me have his daughter. You must know Cabrol, the old man who sweeps up the market? He couldn't think what to do with Rose. I'm teaching her some cooking."

The maid left the room.

"How old is she?" enquired the adjutant.

"Just seventeen. She's stupid and dirty but I only give her ten francs a month and she doesn't eat anything but soup."

When Rose came back with a pile of plates, Laguitte, who was not much interested in girls, followed her with his eyes, surprised at her ugliness. She was short, very swarthy, and slightly humpbacked, with a face like a monkey's, the nose squashed flat, a broad slit of a mouth and narrow, glassy, greenish-coloured eyes. She was broad in the beam, long-armed and looked very strong.

"Heavens above! What a phizog," said Laguitte with a grin when the maid had left the room again in search of salt and pepper.

"Ah well," sighed Burle unconcernedly, "she's very obliging, she does everything she's asked. After all, it's all you need to do the washing-up."

They had a very pleasant meal. There was some beef broth and mutton stew. Charles was encouraged to talk about his life at school. To show what a good boy he was, Madame Burle asked him several times: "You do want to be a soldier, don't you, Charles?" And a smile came to her pale lips when the lad replied with the cowed obedience of a trained dog: "Yes, Grandmamma." Burle had put his elbows on the table and was munching gently, absorbed in his own thoughts. There was a cosy atmosphere round the table, lit by a single lamp which left the corners of the immense room half in darkness. It was an air of comfortable lethargy, the friendly informality of people who are not very well off, who don't bother to change plates for every course, and who feel a thrill of surprise when a bowl of whipped whites of egg and cream custard appears on the table, as a treat, for pudding.

Rose, whose heavy-heeled tread was making the table rock as she walked round the room, had not once opened her mouth while she was serving but now, standing behind Burle, she said in a hoarse voice:

"Would you like cheese, sir?"

Burle gave a start: "What's that? Oh, cheese, yes, hold the plate tightly."

He cut himself a piece of Gruyère while the girl stood watching him through her narrow eyes. Laguitte was laughing to himself. He had been amused by Rose ever since the meal began. Lowering his voice, he whispered in Burle's ear:

"I think she's wonderful, you know. Fancy having a nose and a mouth like that... Why don't you send her round to the colonel one day, so that he can see her. It'll cheer him up!"

He beamed at her ugly face in an avuncular fashion and, wanting to be able to look more closely at her, he said:

"And how about me, my girl? I'd like some cheese too."

She came over with the plate and, sticking his knife into the cheese, he so far forgot his manners as to laugh as he looked at her, when he discovered that one of her nostrils was larger than the other. Rose stolidly allowed herself to be stared at, waiting until the gentleman had stopped laughing.

She cleared the table and disappeared. While the adjutant and Madame Burle continued to chat, the captain dropped off to sleep at once beside the fire. Charles had gone back to his homework. Peace hovered over the room, the peace of a bourgeois family gathered together in good fellowship in the same room. At nine o'clock Burle woke up, yawned and announced that he was going to bed; he was sorry but he just couldn't keep his eyes open. When Laguitte left half an hour later, Madame Burle was unable to find Rose to light his way to the door: she must have already gone to her room; she was like a hen, that girl, she could sleep like a log for twelve hours at a stretch.

"Don't bother to disturb anyone," the adjutant said on the landing, "my legs aren't much better than yours but if I hold on to the banisters, I shan't break anything... Well, I'm a very happy man. All your troubles are over now. I've been watching Burle and I promise you he's not up to any mischief... Damn it all, it really was time for him to give up chasing skirts. It would have led to trouble."

19

The adjutant went on his way delighted at having seen a house of such thoroughly nice people – and they were all living on top of each other, there was no chance of any hanky-panky there!

The thing that really pleased him in this sudden conversion was that he no longer had to check Burle's accounts: there was nothing more boring than all that paperwork. Now that Burle was settling down, all he had to do was smoke his pipe and countersign everything, without a second thought. Even so, he did keep half an eye on the books, but he found the receipts all in order, the totals all balancing correctly – no irregularity at all. After a month, he merely leafed through the receipts and checked the totals, as, indeed, he always had done. But that morning, without any suspicion and purely because he happened to be lighting his pipe at the time, his eyes lingered over an addition and he noticed a mistake of thirteen francs; the total had been increased by thirteen francs to make the account balance. There had been no mistake in the actual figures, because he compared them with the receipts. This struck him as rather suspicious. He did not mention the matter to Burle but promised himself to keep a check on the additions. The following week, another mistake: nineteen francs short. He was so worried by this that he sent for all the ledgers, shut himself up in his office and spent one horrible morning checking everything, every sum, cursing and sweating, his mind reeling with figures. In each total, there were a few francs short: it was a paltry theft, ten francs here, eight francs there, eleven francs and, in the most recent accounts, the figure had even dropped to three or four francs, while in one case Burle had stolen only one and a half francs. So for the last two months, Burle had been nibbling away at the cash in the till. By comparing dates, the adjutant was able to ascertain that the famous "lesson" he had received had kept him straight for barely a week. This was the last straw. He exploded:

"Christ Al-bloody-mighty!" he bellowed, alone in his office, banging the ledgers with his fist, "That's an even dirtier trick!... At least Gagneux's false receipts showed some guts... and now he's sunk to the level of a cook trying to make a few sous on the sly with a saucepanful of stew... Cooking the totals, for Christ's sake!... Buggering about with one franc fifty!... God Almighty! You might at least show some pride, you bastard! Make off with the whole till and blue it on some actress!"

It was the shabby meanness of all these thefts that made him so angry. In addition, he was furious at having been taken in yet again by those false totals, such an obvious and stupid way of cheating. He stood up and paced up and down his room for a whole hour, beside himself with rage, not knowing what to do and talking to himself out loud.

"One thing's for sure, everybody knows what he's like. I must do something... Even if I ticked him off good and proper every morning, he'd still stick a couple of francs in his pocket every afternoon... But what's he spending it on, for Christ's sake? He's stopped going out at night, he's in bed by nine o'clock every evening and everything looks so fair, square, and above board at home... Has the bastard got some other nasty habit we haven't yet discovered?"

He sat down at his desk and totted up the amounts that were missing. They came to five hundred and forty-five francs. Where could they find that money? The annual audit was coming round shortly; it only needed that old fusspot of a colonel to take it into his head to check a total for the whole thing to be discovered. This time, Burle was sunk.

This thought made him feel calmer. He stopped swearing but a chill came over him as the stiff, despairing image of Madame Burle crossed his mind. At the same time, his heart was so full on his own account that he could hardly breathe.

"Come on," he muttered to himself, "the first thing to do is to see exactly how things stand with that bugger. There'll still be time to do something afterwards."

He went round to Burle's office. From across the road he caught a glimpse of a skirt disappearing through a half-open door. Thinking that here was the key to the mystery, he crept quietly up to the door and listened. He at once recognized Mélanie's high-pitched voice, so characteristic of big women. She was complaining about the "sofa-room gentlemen" and mentioned an IOU that she couldn't see how she was going to pay; the bailiffs were in and everything was going to be sold up. Then, as the captain scarcely bothered to reply, saying that he hadn't a penny, she finally burst into tears and called him "Mummy's little darling". But, despite every endearment, she was obviously unable to get round him because all that Burle would say, in a firm, unsympathetic voice, was: "Out of the question. Out of the question." After an hour, she swept out in a fury. Astonished at the turn things were taking, the adjutant waited for a second before going

21

into the room where the captain was sitting alone. He found him quite calm and, resisting the temptation to call him a double-dyed bastard, Laguitte kept his own counsel, anxious to discover the truth first.

There was nothing sinister to be seen in the office. A solid round leather cushion lay on the cane seat of the armchair placed in front of the dark wood table and in a corner stood the cash box, firmly shut. Summer was coming on and the song of a canary floated through the open window. Everything was spick and span and the cardboard boxes were giving off their reassuring smell of old documents.

"Wasn't it that bitch Mélanie that I saw going out as I came in?" enquired Laguitte.

Burle shrugged his shoulders and replied quietly:

"Yes, it was. She was after me again trying to squeeze a couple of hundred francs out of me... She won't get ten, she won't even get ten sous!"

"Won't she?" the other man replied, trying to sound him. "I heard that you'd started seeing her again."

"Me? Good God no! I've had enough of cows like that."

Laguitte took his leave, completely mystified. Where on earth were those five hundred and forty-five francs going? Could the old reprobate have taken to drink or gambling now that he'd given up women? He made up his mind to take Burle by surprise that very evening, so as to be able to question his mother as well and perhaps manage to worm the truth out of him. That afternoon, his leg was hurting atrociously; he had been having a lot of trouble recently and had had to resign himself to taking to a stick to avoid limping too obviously. It irked him dreadfully and he would say, with a mixture of sorrow and anger, that he now really was a disabled soldier. Nevertheless, that evening he made the effort and, hauling himself out of his armchair, he dragged himself to the Rue des Récollets, leaning heavily on his stick under cover of darkness. It was striking nine as he arrived. The street door was ajar and he made his way up. He was on the third floor landing, taking a breather, when he was surprised to hear voices from the floor above. He thought he could recognize Burle's voice and so, out of curiosity, he went on upstairs. On the left, at the end of the corridor, he could see a ray of light coming from a doorway, but his boots creaked, the door was shut and he found himself in complete darkness.

"It's idiotic," he thought to himself. "It must be the cook going to bed."

All the same, approaching as quietly as he could, he put his ear to the door. He could hear two voices and his jaw dropped: it was that bastard Burle and that hideous monster Rose.

"You promised me three francs," she was saying. "Let me have them."

"I'll give you them tomorrow, my little darling," the captain replied beseechingly. "I couldn't manage it today. You know I always keep my promises."

"No, give me my three francs now or else I'll send you packing downstairs."

She must have got undressed already and been sitting on her trestle bed because it creaked every time she moved. The captain could be heard shifting from one foot to another like a cat on hot bricks. He went up to the bed:

"Do be a kind girl. Make room for me."

"Leave me alone!" exclaimed Rose in her grating voice. "I'll scream, I'll tell the old girl downstairs everything… Just hand over the three francs!"

She was insisting on her three francs with the stubbornness of a mule.

Burle lost his temper, then he wept, and finally he took a pot of jam out of his pocket, stolen from his mother's larder. Rose seized hold of it and, without bothering about bread, immediately started digging into it with the handle of a fork which was lying on top of her chest of drawers. It was good jam but when the captain thought he had succeeded in placating her, she pushed him away again as stubbornly as ever.

"You can stuff your jam. I want three francs!"

At this last demand, speechless with rage, the adjutant lifted his stick, ready to split open the door. Christ Almighty! What a bitch! And think of a captain in the French army standing for such a thing! He forgot all about Burle's nasty tricks, he could have strangled that horrible little skivvy for her behaviour. Fancy trying to bargain with an ugly mug like that! It was she who ought to be paying the captain. But he restrained himself, to hear what was going to happen.

"You're making me miserable," the captain was saying, "and when I've been so nice to you… I've given you a dress and some earrings and then a little watch… You don't even use my presents."

"So what? Just to spoil them?... My Dad looks after all my things for me."

"And what about all the money you've got out of me?"

"Dad's investing it for me."

There was silence. Rose was thinking.

"Look, if you swear that you'll let me have six francs tomorrow night, I'll agree... So kneel down and swear you'll bring me six francs. No, you must get down on your knees."

A shudder ran through the adjutant and he moved away from the door to lean against the wall. His legs were giving way under him and in the pitch-dark staircase he was brandishing his stick like a sabre. Good God Almighty! Now he could understand why that bastard Burle was staying home all the time and going to bed at nine o'clock! So that was his wonderful change of heart, by Christ! And with a revolting little trollop that the most depraved of troopers wouldn't have touched with a bargepole!

"For God's sake," said the adjutant out loud, "why didn't he stick to Mélanie?"

What was to be done now? Go in and give the pair of them a taste of his stick? That was his first thought; then he took pity on the old lady downstairs. The best thing was to leave them to their rutting. You'd never get Burle to behave decently. When a man sank as low as that, the only thing to do was to throw a spadeful of mud over him and get rid of him like the rotting carcass of some poisonous beast. And even if you shoved his nose in his own shit, he'd only start again the next day and end up stealing a few sous to buy sticks of barley sugar for lice-ridden little beggar girls. Christ Almighty! And it was money belonging to the French army! And what about the honour of the flag? And the respectable name of Burle that would end up in the gutter! Christ Almighty! It mustn't end like that!

For a moment the adjutant half relented. If only he had those five hundred and forty-five francs! But he hadn't got a brass farthing. Yesterday evening, after getting drunk like any subaltern, he'd lost an enormous sum at cards. He deserved to have to limp! He ought to have been killed!

So he left the loathsome couple to their antics and went downstairs to ring at Madame Burle's door. After a good five minutes, the old lady herself came to open it.

"I'm sorry," she said. "I thought that sleepyhead Rose was still here... I must go and give her a shake in bed."

The adjutant stopped her.

"What about Burle?" he asked.

"Oh, he's been snoring away ever since nine o'clock. Would you like me to go and knock on his door?"

"No, please don't do that... All I wanted is a little evening chat with you."

In the dining room Charles was sitting in his usual place at the table and had just finished his Latin translation. But he had a terrified look on his face and his hands were trembling. Before sending him off to bed, his grandmother would read him accounts of famous battles, in order to stimulate his sense of pride in family heroism. That evening, the story of the *Avenger*, a ship full of dead and wounded which went to the bottom in the midst of the ocean, had left the little boy in a dreadful state of nerves, his head whirling with horrible nightmare visions.

Madame Burle asked Laguitte to let her finish reading the story. Then, as the last sailor shouted: "Long live the Republic!", she solemnly shut the book. Charles was as white as a sheet.

"You heard that, didn't you?" the old lady said. "It's the duty of every French soldier to die for his country."

"Yes, Grandma."

He kissed her on the forehead and went off to bed, trembling with fear, in the vast room where the slightest creak in the woodwork brought him out in a cold sweat.

The adjutant had been listening earnestly. Yes, by God, honour was honour and he must never let that scoundrel Burle bring dishonour on that poor old woman and the young lad. Since the youngster had such a liking for military life, he must be able to get into Saint-Cyr, holding his head high. But the adjutant was still trying to dismiss from his mind a dreadful thought which had been troubling him ever since the mention of those six francs upstairs when Madame Burle picked up the lamp to show him out. As they walked past the captain's bedroom, she was surprised to see the key in the door, something she had never seen before.

"Come in," she said, "it's bad for him to sleep so much, it makes him lethargic."

And before he could stop her, she pushed open the door and stood rooted to the spot when she saw that the room was empty. Laguitte had gone very red and he looked so foolish that all at once dozens of little details fell into place in her mind and she realized the truth.

"You knew about it, you knew all about it," she stammered.

"Why didn't you warn me? Heavens above, in my own house, with his son sleeping in the next room... and with that scullery maid, that hideous-looking scullery maid!... And he's been stealing again, I can feel it in my bones!"

She stood there, white-faced and rigid. Then she added harshly: "I wish he were dead!"

Laguitte took hold of her two hands and clasped them tightly for a second in his own. Then he quickly took his leave, for he had a lump in his throat and he would have burst into tears. Christ Almighty! This time his mind really was made up!

4

THE AUDIT WAS DUE TO TAKE PLACE at the end of the month. The adjutant still had ten days to act. The very next day he limped his way to the Café de Paris, where he ordered a beer. Mélanie had gone very pale and Phrosyne took him his beer very reluctantly, fully expecting to have her face slapped. But the adjutant seemed very relaxed; he asked for a chair to rest his leg on and then drank his beer like any honest thirsty citizen. He had been sitting there an hour when he saw two brother officers crossing the square, the battalion commander Morandot and Captain Doucet.

"Come and have a drink," he called out to them when they were in earshot.

The officers could hardly refuse. When the little barmaid had served them, Morandot asked:

"So you come here now, do you?"

Captain Doucet gave a knowing wink.

"Have you become one of the 'sofa-room gents'?"

Laguitte merely laughed. Then they started pulling his leg about Mélanie, whereupon he gave a good-natured shrug of his shoulders; she was a fine figure of a woman, when all was said and done, and though people were very ready to make jokes about her, those who were prepared to run her down would still have been quite glad of a nibble. Then he turned towards the bar and, making his voice as affable as possible, he called out:

"Three more beers please, Madame Mélanie!"

Mélanie was so surprised that she stood up and fetched the beers herself. When she came to the table, the major engaged her in conversation, even going so far as to give her a gentle tap or two on her hand which was resting on the back of one of the chairs. At this, Mélanie herself, used to getting both kicks and ha'pence, began to flirt with the major, imagining that she had attracted the fancy of the old cripple, as she used to call him privately when talking with Phrosyne. Doucet and Morandot were exchanging glances. Well! Well! Damned if their old adjutant wasn't following in Skirty's footsteps! The regiment would certainly enjoy that!

Meanwhile Laguitte had been keeping one eye on the Place du Palais through the open door and now he suddenly exclaimed:

"I say, there's Burle!"

"Yes, this is the time he goes by," said Mélanie, also coming to look. "He comes this way every afternoon when he leaves the office."

Despite his bad leg, the adjutant had jumped to his feet and, pushing his way through the chairs, he shouted:

"Hullo, Burle! Come and have a beer!"

The captain was quite taken aback and wondered how Laguitte came to be at Mélanie's with Doucet and Morandot. However, he automatically came over and stood, still hesitating, in the doorway.

The adjutant ordered a beer and then, turning round, he said:

"What on earth's the matter?... Come in and sit down. Do you think somebody's going to eat you?"

When the captain had come in and sat down, there was a moment of embarrassment. As she brought the glass of beer, Mélanie's hands were trembling slightly, for she was in constant fear that there would be a row which would lead to the closing of her establishment. She now felt worried by the adjutant's amiability and was just trying to slip away when Laguitte invited her to have a drink with the gentlemen, and, acting as if he owned the place, he had already ordered a glass of anisette. Mélanie found herself forced to sit down between him and the captain. The adjutant kept saying, in a bullying tone:

"I insist that these ladies be shown respect!... For heaven's sake, let's behave like gentlemen! We'll drink Mélanie's health!"

Burle was looking at his glass with an embarrassed smile on his face. Shocked at the toast, the two other officers were trying to stand up and leave. Fortunately, the room was empty, with only the usual group of players having their customary game of dominoes who kept looking meaningfully at each other each time they heard an oath; so scandalized were they at seeing so many people in the room that they were thinking of taking their game to the Café de la Gare if the military were going to invade their private domain. The only other occupants were a whole swarm of buzzing flies, attracted by the filth of the tables which Phrosyne nowadays bothered to wash only on Saturdays; she herself had gone back to her novel which she was reading sprawled out behind the bar.

"Well? Aren't you going to drink Madame Mélanie's health?" snapped the adjutant to Burle. "You might at least show some manners!"

And as Doucet and Morandot once more stood up to leave:

"Wait a second, for God's sake! I'm coming with you. The trouble is that that brute there has never known how to behave!"

The two officers stood there, amazed at the adjutant's sudden outburst. Mélanie, trying to smooth matters down, laid a restraining hand on the two men's arms and gave a soothing laugh.

"No, leave me alone! Why wouldn't he drink your health? I'm not going to allow you to be insulted, do you understand?... I'm fed up to the teeth with this pig!"

At this insult, Burle went white to the teeth and, standing up, said to Morandot:

"What's the matter with him? He's invited me here to create a row... Is he drunk?"

"Damn and blast your eyes!" bellowed Laguitte.

And, rising to his feet on his trembling legs, he leant over and gave the captain a resounding slap across the face. Mélanie barely had time to duck to avoid receiving some of it on her own ear. There was a dreadful commotion. Phrosyne started to scream as if it were she who had been hit. The terrified domino players took refuge behind their table, imagining that all these soldiers were about to draw their sabres and hack each other to pieces. Meanwhile Morandot and Doucet had caught hold of the captain by his arms to prevent him from hurling himself on the adjutant and were leading him gently towards the door.

Once outside, they succeeded in calming him down a little by putting all the blame on to Laguitte. The colonel would pass judgement, because they would go and see him to tell him all about the affair that very evening, since they had been witnesses. When they had persuaded Burle to leave, they went back into the café where Laguitte, in a very emotional state and close to tears, was pretending to be calm as he finished off his beer.

"Look here, Laguitte," Major Morandot said, "this is a very bad business. The captain isn't of equal rank with you and you know very well that it's impossible for him to be granted permission to fight you."

"We'll see about that!" retorted the adjutant.

"But what did he do to you? He wasn't even talking to you... Two old comrades like you, it's absurd!"

Laguitte made a vague gesture.

"Never mind! He was getting on my nerves."

That was all he would say and no one was ever any the wiser. All the same, it caused a tremendous stir. The general opinion in the regiment was that Mélanie, furious at having been dropped by the captain, had succeeded in getting her claws in Laguitte and by retailing horrific stories about Burle had persuaded the adjutant to slap the captain's face. Who would ever have credited it, of that hardened old sinner Laguitte, after all the dreadful things he used to say about women. Well, it'd been his turn to be curbed. Despite the general revulsion against Mélanie, this adventure set her up as a woman to be reckoned with, a woman to be both feared and desired, and henceforth her establishment was to flourish greatly.

The following day, the colonel sent for the adjutant and the captain. He gave them both a sharp dressing down, accusing them of bringing the army into disrepute in a notorious place. What did they intend to do about it now, since he could not possibly authorize them to fight? This was the question which had kept the whole regiment on tenterhooks ever since the previous day. An apology seemed to be excluded because of the slap in the face; however, since Laguitte could hardly stand because of his bad leg, it was felt that a reconciliation might be brought about if the colonel insisted.

"Well now," the colonel went on, "are you both prepared to let me act as arbitrator?"

"Excuse me, colonel," the adjutant interposed, "I wish to resign my commission... Here's my resignation. I think that settles everything. Will you please fix the day for the duel?"

Burle looked at him in surprise. For his part, the colonel felt that he should make some observations of his own:

"That's a very serious decision you're making, Laguitte... You've only two years to go before retirement."

The adjutant broke in again:

"That's my concern," he said gruffly.

"Well, yes, certainly... Very well then, I'll forward your resignation and as soon as it's approved, I'll fix the day for the duel."

The outcome of this interview stunned the regiment. What on earth had got into their crazy adjutant to make him want to risk getting his throat cut by his old comrade Burle? Mélanie's name was again mentioned and her being such a fine figure of a woman; all the officers had by now become obsessed by her and intrigued by the thought that she must be a really hot bit of stuff to make those two tough old campaigners lose their heads in that way. The battalion commander, Major Morandot, happening to meet Laguitte, made no secret of his concern. Assuming he wasn't killed, what was he going to live on? He had no private means and he'd have a job to afford anything better than dry bread on the pension he'd get from his decoration and his half-pay. While Morandot was speaking, Laguitte said not a word but stared vacantly into space, completely oblivious to anything apart from his own dogged obsessions. Then, when the other man tried to discover the reasons for his hatred of Burle, he merely repeated his former phrase, accompanied by the same vague gesture:

"He was getting on my nerves. Never mind!"

Every morning, in the barrack room and in the mess, the first question was: "Well, has his resignation come through yet?" Everyone was awaiting the duel and above all discussing its probable outcome. Most people thought that Laguitte would be run through in a couple of seconds because it was absurd to want to fight at his age, with a gammy leg that wouldn't even allow him to lunge. A few people, however, shook their heads knowingly: true, Laguitte had never been a genius; indeed, for the last twenty years his name had been a password for stupidity, but in the old days, he was known as the best swordsman in the regiment, and, brought up in the military school, he had risen from the ranks to become a battalion commander through his extreme bravery and complete disregard of danger. Burle, on the other hand, was a very ordinary swordsman and had the reputation of being a coward. Anyway, they'd all have to wait and see. And excitement grew as that confounded resignation was an interminable time coming through.

The man who was most worried and upset was certainly the adjutant: a week had already passed and the general audit was due to start the day after tomorrow. There was still no news. He was appalled by the thought that he might have slapped his old friend's face and sent in his resignation for nothing, without holding back the scandal for a single minute. If he were to be killed, however, at least he would be spared the aggravation of knowing about it, and if he killed Burle, as he was relying on doing, they would hush the matter up at once: he would have saved the honour of the army and the youngster would get into Saint-Cyr. But those miserable pen-pushers at the Ministry would have to get a move on, blast their eyes! The adjutant was on tenterhooks: he could be seen lurking around the post office, looking out for each delivery, questioning the colonel's duty orderly, in order to find out what was happening. He spent sleepless nights and took to his stick, no longer caring what people might think when they saw him limping heavily.

On the day before the audit, Laguitte was making his way yet again to the colonel when he was dismayed to see Madame Burle who was taking Charles to school. He had not seen her since his last visit and she, for her part, had shut herself up in her flat in the Rue des Récollets. Almost in a state of collapse, he moved over to leave the whole pavement free for her and the boy. Neither of them greeted the other, which made the little boy open his eyes wide in astonishment. Stiff as a ramrod, Madame Burle brushed coldly past without the quiver of an eyelid. And when she had gone by, he looked after her with eyes full of bewilderment.

"For Christ's sake," he grunted, forcing back his tears, "don't tell me I'm becoming a woman!"

As he was going in to see the colonel, a captain in the office said:

"Well, that's it! Your papers have come through."

"Ah!" he murmured, white as a sheet.

He could still see in his mind's eye that stiff and implacable old lady walking away holding her grandson's hand. Good God! To think that he had been awaiting the arrival of those papers so anxiously for the last week and now they had come he felt all upset and excited!

The duel took place next morning behind a low wall in the barrack yard. It was a bright sunny day, with a nip in the air. Laguitte had almost to be carried to the spot. One of his seconds gave him his arm while he supported himself on his stick with the other. Burle, whose yellow unhealthy-looking face was bloated with fat, was walking as if in a dream, like someone benumbed by a night of debauchery. Not a word was exchanged. Everyone wanted to put an end to the proceedings with all possible speed.

Captain Doucet, who was one of the seconds, engaged the swords, stood back and said:

"Go ahead, gentlemen!"

Burle attacked at once, in order to put Laguitte to the test and see what he might expect. For the last few days he had been living in a nightmare world of absurdity, unable to understand what was happening. He did, indeed, suspect something but he rejected this suspicion with a shudder for he could see death at the end of it and refused to believe that a friend could play such a macabre joke on him in order to settle such a matter. Moreover, Laguitte's leg gave him a certain confidence. He would prick him in the shoulder and there the matter would end.

For nearly two minutes the swords clinked and scraped together, steel against steel. Then the captain disengaged and attempted to lunge, but the adjutant, his wrist suddenly discovering its strength of earlier days, made a fierce parry "in quinte" and, had the captain tried to counter, he would have been pierced through and through. Hastily, he broke off, ghastly pale as he felt himself at the mercy of this man who, for this once, had let him off. He was, at last, beginning to understand: this was an execution.

However, planted firmly on his bad legs, Laguitte, solid as a rock, was biding his time. The two opponents were staring at each other. Into Burle's baffled gaze there came an imploring look, a plea for mercy: he knew that he was about to die and, like a naughty child, he was promising never to do it again. But in the adjutant's eyes there was no spark of pity; honour was at stake and he must stifle any feeling of compassion that might be prompted by his own good nature.

"Let's finish if off!" he muttered to himself.

This time it was he who attacked. There was a flash of steel as his sword darted from right to left and back again and then like a streak of lightning planted itself straight in the captain's chest. He fell like a log, without a sound.

Laguitte let go of his sword and looked down at that poor bastard Burle lying flat on his back with his pot belly up in the air. He kept repeating, in an angry, broken voice:

"Christ Almighty! Christ Almighty!"

They led him away. Both his legs were affected and his seconds had to support him on both sides, for he was unable even to use his stick.

Two months later, the former adjutant was limping painfully in the sun along a deserted street in Vauchamp when he again met Madame Burle and young Charles. They were both dressed in deep mourning. He tried to avoid them but he had difficulty in walking and they were coming straight towards him, not altering their pace in the slightest. Charles still had his gentle, scared, girlish expression. Madame Burle, unbending as ever, was looking harsher and more gaunt. As Laguitte stepped sideways into a carriage gateway, leaving the whole street clear for them, she suddenly stopped in front of him and held out her hand. He hesitated, then finally put out his own and shook it, but he was trembling so much that he made the old lady's arm shake. They looked each other in the eyes without a word.

"Charles," said his grandmother at last, "shake hands with Major Laguitte."

The child obeyed, without understanding. The major had gone as white as a sheet. He could hardly bring himself to touch the little boy's frail fingers. Then, realizing that he ought to say something, the only thing he could think of was:

"You're still hoping to send him to Saint-Cyr?"

"Certainly, when he's old enough."

Next week, Charles was carried off by typhoid. One evening, pursuing her policy of making him tough, his grandmother had once more read him the heroic story of the *Avenger*. That night, he became delirious. In fact, he had died of fright.

Coqueville on the Spree*

1

C OQUEVILLE IS A LITTLE VILLAGE snuggling down in a rocky inlet five
miles from Grandport. A fine broad sandy beach stretches out at
the foot of the ramshackle old cottages stuck halfway up the cliff-face
like shells left high and dry by the tide. When you climb to the left,
up on to the heights of Grandport, you can see the yellow expanse of
beach very plainly to the west, looking like a tide of gold dust flowing
out of the gaping slit in the rock, and if you have good eyes, you can
even make out the tumbledown cottages standing out, rust-coloured
against the stone, with the bluish smoke from their chimneys drifting
upwards to the crest of the enormous ridge blocking the horizon.

It's an out-of-the-way hole. Coqueville has never succeeded in bringing
its population up to the two hundred mark. The gorge running down
to the sea, on the edge of which the village is situated, is so steep and
winding that it is almost impassable for horses and carts. This prevents
communication and isolates the village so that it seems miles away
from any of the neighbouring hamlets. As a result, the inhabitants'
only communication with Grandport was by water. They were almost
all fishermen living from the sea and had to transport their catch there
by boat every day. They had a contract with a large firm of wholesalers,
Dufeu's, which bought their fish in bulk. Old Dufeu had been dead
for some years but the business had been carried on by his widow; she
had merely taken on an assistant, a tall fair-headed young fellow called
Mouchel, whose job was to visit the villages along the coast and strike
bargains with the villagers. This Monsieur Mouchel was the only link
between Coqueville and the civilized world.

Coqueville deserves to have a historian. It seems certain that in
the Dark Ages the village was founded by the Mahés, a family which
found its way there, settled down and proliferated at the foot of the
cliff. At first, the Mahés must have flourished by intermarriage, since
for centuries you find nothing but Mahés. Then, under Louis XIII,*

there appeared a Floche. No one really knows where he came from. He married a Mahé and from that moment onwards a strange phenomenon occurred: the Floches prospered and were so prolific that they ended up by engulfing the Mahés, whose numbers decreased while their wealth passed into the newcomers' hands. Doubtless the Floches had brought new blood, a sturdier constitution and a temperament more suited to face the strong winds and rough seas of their profession. However that might be, the Floches were by now the bosses of Coqueville.

You will have realized that this shift in numbers and wealth had not taken place without terrible strife. The Mahés and the Floches hated each other like poison; centuries of loathing seethed between them. Despite their decline, the Mahés were proud, as befitted a former conqueror. After all, they were the founders and ancestors. They would speak with scorn of the first of the Floches, a beggar and a tramp whom they had taken into their bosoms out of pity, and they expressed eternal regret at having given him one of their daughters. If you were to believe them, this Floche had produced nothing but a breed of lewd rogues who spent their nights in copulation and their days in pursuit of heiresses. There was no insult too foul to heap on the powerful tribe of Floches, with the bitter fury of ruined and decimated aristocrats against the arrogant and prolific middle classes who had dispossessed them of their mansions and their wealth that were theirs by right of inheritance. Needless to say, success had turned the Floches, on their part, into an arrogant lot. They were sitting pretty and could afford to sneer. They made fun of the ancient race of Mahé and swore to turn them out of the village if they didn't knuckle under. For them, the Mahés were down-and-outs who, instead of wrapping themselves proudly in their tattered finery, would be better employed mending it. Thus Coqueville found itself the prey of two warring clans; about one hundred and thirty of its inhabitants determined to take over the other fifty, for no other reason than that they were stronger. Struggles between mighty empires tell the same story.

Amongst the recent squabbles which had been tearing Coqueville apart, we may mention the famous feud between Fouasse and Tupain and the spectacular brawls between the Rouget couple. It must be explained that in the old days everyone was given a nickname, which later on became a surname, because it was difficult to disentangle all the cross-breedings of Mahé and Floche. Rouget had certainly once had an ancestor who had flaming red hair; as for Fouasse and Tupain, no one knew the reason for their names, since in the course of the years many nicknames had lost any rational explanation. Well, old Françoise, a sprightly old girl of eighty, still alive, had married a Mahé and produced Fouasse; then, after being widowed, had remarried a Floche and given birth to Tupain. Hence the mutual antagonism of the two brothers, a hatred kept alive by the fact that questions of inheritance were involved. As for the Rougets, they fought like cat and dog because Rouget accused his wife Marie of carrying on with a dark-haired Floche, the tall and sturdy Brisemotte.* Rouget had already flung himself a couple of times on the latter, knife in hand, screaming that he would have his guts for garters. He was an excitable little man, always flying into rages.

But Coqueville's major concern at the moment was neither Rouget's rages nor Tupain's and Fouasse's squabbles. There was a wild rumour going round that a Mahé, Delphin, a whippersnapper of twenty, had the audacity to be in love with Margot, the beautiful daughter of La Queue, the wealthiest of the Floches and mayor of the village. This La Queue was a very considerable person indeed. He was called La Queue because under Louis Philippe, his father, obstinately clinging to fashions prevalent in his youth, had been the last man in the village to tie his hair in a pigtail.* Now La Queue owned *Zephyr*, one of Coqueville's two large fishing boats and by far the best, a fine seaworthy vessel, newly built. The other cutter was the *Whale*, a rotten old tub owned by Rouget and manned by Delphin and Fouasse, while La Queue sailed with a crew consisting of Tupain and Brisemotte. The latter were always making sarcastic comments about the *Whale*, describing it as an old tub which, one fine day, would disintegrate like a handful of mud. So when La Queue heard that this good-for-nothing young Delphin, the *Whale*'s cabin boy, was daring to make sheep's eyes at his daughter, he gave her a couple of well-directed slaps in the face as a warning that she would never become a Mahé. Margot was furious and responded by loudly proclaiming that she would pass on the same treatment to Delphin if he ever had the nerve to start prowling around her. It was maddening to have your ears boxed because of a young man whom you'd never really bothered to look at properly. Although only sixteen, Margot was as strong as a man and already as lovely as

37

any lady; she had the reputation of being high and mighty, a young madam who had no time for sweethearts. So you can well understand how those two slaps, Delphin's audacity and Margot's anger had kept every tongue wagging in Coqueville.

However, there were people who said that Margot was not as angry as all that at seeing Delphin hanging around her. This Delphin was a small young fellow with a face tanned by the sea and a mop of blond curls that hung down over his eyes and neck. And, despite his slender build, he was very strong and quite capable of tackling someone three times his size. Rumour had it that he would sometimes go off and spend the night in Grandport. This gave him a reputation with the girls of being something of a wolf, and when talking together they would accuse him of "living it up", a vague phrase which suggested all kinds of secret pleasures. Whenever she mentioned his name, Margot seemed to become rather too excited, while when he looked at her through his tiny bright eyes, he would give a sly grin and show not the slightest concern whether she was angry or scornful. He would walk past her front door, slip into the bushes and stay watching her for hours, as lithe and patient as a cat stalking a tomtit, and when she suddenly discovered him right behind her, so close at times that she would detect his presence by the warmth of his breath, he did not take himself off but would put on such a gentle, wistful look that she was left speechless with surprise and remembered to be annoyed only after he had gone. There is no doubt that, had her father seen her, she would have collected another box on the ears. Things could certainly not go on like this for ever, but although she kept swearing that one day she would give Delphin the promised box on the ears, she never in fact took advantage of any opportunity of doing so when he was there. This made people say that she'd do better not to keep on talking so much about it, since the truth was that she still had given no sign of keeping her word.

All the same, nobody ever imagined that she would ever marry Delphin. It seemed merely a case of a passing fancy by a flirtatious young girl. As for marriage between the most poverty-stricken of the Mahés, who would find it hard to contribute even half a dozen shirts to the matrimonial estate, and the mayor's daughter, the richest heiress among the Floches, the whole idea would be monstrous. Unkind people hinted that she might nonetheless quite possibly get together with him but that she would certainly never marry him. A rich girl can enjoy herself as she pleases but when she has her head screwed on straight, she doesn't do anything silly. Anyway, the whole of Coqueville was taking a passionate interest in the matter and was curious to see the outcome. Would Delphin end up getting his ears boxed? Or would Margot get a kiss on her cheek in some remote corner of the cliffs? They'd have to wait and see. Some people supported the box on the ears, others the kiss on the cheek. Coqueville was all agog.

In the whole village there were only two people who did not belong either to the Mahé or the Floche camps: the priest and the gamekeeper. The latter, a tall lean man whose real name no one knew but whom everyone called the Emperor,* doubtless because he had served under Charles X, in fact exercised no serious supervision whatsoever over the game of the district, which consisted of nothing but bare rock and deserted heathland. He had got the job because a *sous-préfet** had taken him under his wing and had created on his behalf this sinecure where he was free to squander his very modest salary undisturbed. As for Father Radiguet, he was one of those simple-minded priests whom bishops are anxious to get rid of by tucking them away in some God-forsaken hole where they can stay out of mischief. Radiguet was a decent sort of man who had reverted to his peasant origins and spent his time working in his exiguous little garden hewn out of the rock-face, and smoking his pipe as he watched his lettuces grow. His only weakness was a love of food, although he was hardly in a position to show a discriminating palate, since he was forced to make do with a diet of mackerel and cider, of which he sometimes drank more than he could hold. All the same, he was a good shepherd to his flock and they would come along, at infrequent intervals, to hear him say mass, purely to oblige him.

However, after managing to remain neutral for a long time, the priest and the gamekeeper had been forced to take sides. Conservative at heart, the Emperor had opted for the Mahés while the priest had become a Flochite. This had given rise to complications. As the Emperor had absolutely nothing to do all day long and was tired of counting the boats leaving Grandport harbour, he had taken it into his head to act as the village policeman. As a Mahé supporter, he favoured Fouasse against Tupain, tried to catch Brisemotte and Rouget's wife red-handed and, above all, turned a blind eye when he saw Delphin slipping into Margot's backyard. The trouble was that these goings-on led to violent disagreement between him and his direct superior, the mayor La Queue. While being sufficiently respectful of discipline to listen to the mayor's rebukes, the gamekeeper would then go away and do as he thought fit, thereby causing complete chaos in Coqueville's public administration. You could never go near the glorified shed that served as Coqueville's town hall without being deafened by the sound of some flaming row or other between the two. Father Radiguet, on the other hand, having joined the triumphant clan of the Floches, who showered him with gifts of superb mackerel, secretly encouraged Rouget's wife to stand up to her husband and threatened Margot with all the torments of hell if she ever let Delphin lay as much as a finger on her. In a word, anarchy reigned supreme, with the army in revolt against the civil authority and religion conniving at the frolics of the wealthier members of his flock, so that, in this dead-and-alive little hole looking out upon the infinite expanse of the sky and the vast sweep of the ocean, you had a whole community of fully one hundred and eighty souls at daggers drawn with each other.

In the midst of all this turmoil, Delphin alone never lost his good spirits; young and in love as he was, he did not give a damn for anything or anybody, as long as Margot would one day be his. He may well have been planning to snare her like a rabbit, but being a sensible lad despite his wild ways, he was going to see to it that the priest should tie the knot that would ensure that they would live happily ever after.

One evening as he was lying in wait for her in a lane, Margot finally took a swing at him and then blushed purple in confusion when, instead of waiting for the blow to land, Delphin caught hold of her hand and feverishly covered it in kisses.

She was trembling as he whispered to her:

"I love you. Will you love me?"

"Never!" she cried in a shocked voice.

He gave a shrug of his shoulders and said quietly, with a tender look in his eyes:

"Please don't say that... We'll get on very well together, the pair of us. You'll see just how nice it is."

2

T HAT SUNDAY, the weather was dreadful, one of those sudden September storms which blow up with terrible force on the rocky coast round Grandport. As dusk was falling, Coqueville caught a glimpse of a vessel in distress being driven before the wind. But the light was failing and there was no question of going to her rescue. Since the previous day, *Zephyr* and the *Whale* had been tied up in the tiny natural harbour to the left of the beach, between the two granite sea walls. Neither La Queue nor Rouget were going to risk venturing out. Unfortunately, Madame Dufeu's representative, Monsieur Mouchel, had taken the trouble to come over personally on Saturday to offer a bonus if they made a real effort: catches were poor and the Central Market was complaining. So when they went to bed on Sunday with the rain still pelting down, the fishermen of Coqueville were bad-tempered and full of grumbles. It was always the same old story: when the demand was good, the fish just weren't there. And they all discussed the ship that had been seen passing during the gale and which by now was no doubt lying at the bottom of the ocean.

Next day the sky was still black and the sea running high, booming and thundering and reluctant to calm down, even though the wind was blowing less strongly. It then dropped completely and though the waves were still rearing and tossing furiously, both boats went out that afternoon. *Zephyr* returned at about four o'clock, having caught nothing. While Tupain and Brisemotte were tying up in the little harbour, La Queue stood on the beach, shaking his fist angrily at the sea. And Monsieur Mouchel was expecting something from them! Margot was there with half of Coqueville, watching the heavy swell of the dying storm and sharing her father's resentment against the sea and the sky.

"Where's the *Whale?*" someone asked.

"Over there, behind the point," replied La Queue. "If that old tub gets back safe and sound today, it'll be lucky."

His voice was full of scorn. He went on to suggest that it was quite understandable for the Mahés to risk their lives like that. When you haven't got two pennies to rub together, you don't have much choice. As for him, he'd sooner let Monsieur Mouchel go begging.

Meanwhile Margot was scrutinizing the rocky point behind which the *Whale* was hidden. Finally she asked her father:

"Did they catch anything?"

"Them!" he exclaimed. "Not a thing!"

Noticing that the Emperor was grinning, he calmed down and added more quietly:

"I don't know if they've caught anything but as they never do…"

"Perhaps they have caught something today after all," said the Emperor teasingly. "It has been known to happen."

La Queue was about to make a heated retort when Father Radiguet arrived and succeeded in soothing him. From the flat top of the church, Radiguet had just caught a glimpse of the *Whale* which seemed to be in pursuit of some large fish. This news created great excitement among the villagers gathered on the beach, with the Mahé supporters hoping for a miraculous catch and the Floches very keen for the boat to come back empty-handed. Margot was craning her neck and looking out to sea.

"There they are!" she exclaimed briefly.

And in fact a black speck could be seen beyond the point.

Everyone looked. It looked like a cork bobbing up and down on the sea. The Emperor could not even see the black speck: you had to be from Coqueville to recognize the *Whale* and its crew at that distance.

"Yes," Margot went on, for she had the best eyes of anyone in the village, "Fouasse and Rouget are rowing and the boy's standing in the bow."

She called Delphin "the boy" to avoid mentioning him by name. Now they were able to follow the course of the boat and try to understand its strange manoeuvres. As the priest had said, it seemed to be pursuing a fish which kept swimming away to escape. It was an extraordinary sight. The Emperor thought that their net had probably been carried away but La Queue exclaimed that they were just being lazy and footling about. They wouldn't be catching seals, that was for sure! The Floches all found this a hilarious remark while the Mahés felt annoyed and pointed out that anyway Rouget had guts and was risking his life while certain other people stuck to dry land at the slightest puff of wind. Once again, Father Radiguet had to intervene because fists were being clenched.

"What on earth are they up to!" exclaimed Margot suddenly. "They've gone again!"

They all stopped glowering at each other and everyone scanned the horizon. Once more the *Whale* was hidden behind the point. This time, even La Queue was becoming uneasy. Since he was unable to explain to himself what they were doing, and fearing that Rouget might really be making a good catch, he was beside himself with rage. No one left the beach even though there was nothing particular to see. They stayed there for two hours, still waiting for the boat which kept appearing and then vanishing. In the end it disappeared altogether. La Queue declared it must have gone to the bottom and in his anger he even found himself wishing in his heart of hearts that this might be true, and as Rouget's wife happened to be present with Brisemotte, he looked at them with a conspiratorial grin and gave Tupain a friendly tap on the shoulder to console him for the loss of his half-brother Fouasse. But he stopped laughing when he saw his daughter Margot on tiptoe peering silently into the distance.

"What do you think you're doing here?" he said gruffly. "Off you go back home... And have a care, Margot!"

She made no move but suddenly called out:

"Look, there they are!"

There was a cry of surprise. With her sharp eyes, Margot swore that she couldn't see a soul on board. No Rouget, no Fouasse, nobody! The *Whale* was running before the wind as though abandoned, changing tack every minute as it bobbed lazily up and down. Fortunately a breeze had sprung up from the west which was driving the boat landwards, in an oddly capricious way, so that it yawed first to port and then to starboard. The whole of Coqueville was by now assembled on the beach. Everybody was calling out to everyone else and there was not a woman or a girl left at home to prepare the supper. It could only be some sort of disaster, something inexplicable and so mysterious that they all felt quite at a loss. Rouget's wife thought quickly and decided that she ought to burst into tears. The most Tupain could do was to look miserable. All the Mahés were looking distressed while the Floches were trying hard to show some decorum. Margot had sat down on the beach as if her legs had suddenly collapsed.

"What on earth are you doing there?" exclaimed La Queue, seeing her at his feet.

"I'm tired," she said simply.

And she turned her head to look out to sea, holding her face in her hands and peering through the tips of her fingers at the *Whale* bobbing up and down even more lazily, like a cheerful boat that has had too much to drink.

Theories were now flying thick and fast. Perhaps the three men had fallen into the sea? But for all three to do that at once seemed very odd. La Queue was trying to persuade people that the *Whale* had split open like a rotten egg. But as she was still afloat, the others merely shrugged their shoulders. Then he remembered that he was mayor and began to talk about various formalities, as if the men were really drowned.

"What's the point of talking like that!" exclaimed the Emperor. "How could people die as stupidly as that? If they'd fallen in, Delphin would have been here by now!"

They all had to agree; Delphin could swim like a fish. But in that case, where on earth could the three men be? Everyone was shouting. "I'm telling you it is!" "And I'm telling you it isn't!" "Stupid!" "Stupid yourself!" And they were getting to the stage of exchanging blows, so that Father Radiguet was forced to make an appeal for the cessation of hostilities while the Emperor hurriedly tried to restore order. Meanwhile the boat continued to bob lazily up and down under everyone's eyes. It was as though she was dancing and laughing at them all and as she drifted in on the tide, she seemed to be greeting the approaching land with a series of slow, rhythmical curtsies. She was a crazy boat, that was for sure!

Margot was still hiding her face and peering through her hands. A rowing boat had just put out from the harbour to go to meet the *Whale*: losing patience, Brisemotte seemed anxious to put an end to Marie Rouget's uncertainty. Now Coqueville's whole attention was focused on the rowing boat. They started shouting: Could he see anything? The *Whale* kept coming on, still looking mysterious and saucy. At last they saw him catch hold of one of the mooring ropes and stand up to look into the boat. Then suddenly he burst into fits of laughter. They were all mystified. What could he see that was so funny?

"Hi there! What's up?" they shouted excitedly. His only reply was to go on laughing even more loudly, making signs that they were soon going to find out. Then he tied the *Whale* to his own boat and towed her in. And the inhabitants of Coqueville were stunned at the extraordinary sight that met their eyes. The three men, Rouget, Fouasse and Delphin, were lying flat on their backs, fast asleep, blissfully snoring and dead drunk. In the middle, there lay a small cask that had been stoved in, a cask that had been full when they had picked it up. They had been drinking from it and it must have been good stuff, because they had drunk it all except for a litre or so that had spilled out into the boat and become mixed with seawater.

"Oh, what a pig!" cried Rouget's wife and stopped snivelling.

"Well, that's a fine catch, I must say," said La Queue, putting on a dignified air.

"Hang on!" said the Emperor. "People catch what they can and after all, they did catch a barrel at least, which is more than those who didn't catch anything."

Piqued by this remark, the mayor said no more. But Coqueville's other inhabitants were commenting excitedly. Now they could understand! When boats get drunk, they prance about, just like human beings, and that boat had certainly had a bellyful! The tipsy old so-and-so! She'd been zigzagging about just like a drunk who couldn't find his way home. And some were laughing at it and some were annoyed, for the Mahés found it funny and the Floches thought it disgusting. They all gathered round the *Whale*, peering open-eyed at the three happy fellows snoring away with smiles all over their faces, completely oblivious to the crowd bending over them. Neither the insults nor the laughter could greatly disturb them. Rouget was unable to hear his wife accusing him of drinking the lot. Fouasse did not feel the sly kicks in his ribs being given him by his brother Tupain. As for Delphin, he looked charming, with his fair hair, pink cheeks and air of rapturous delight. Margot had stood up and was silently contemplating the young man with a hard look in her eyes.

"Better get them to bed!" a voice cried.

But at that very moment, Delphin started to open his eyes and, still with his blissfully happy expression, began to look around at the crowd of people watching him. At once, everybody started questioning him, so excitedly that he felt quite bewildered, especially as he was still as drunk as a lord.

"Well, what's all the fuss?" he stammered. "It's a little cask. There wasn't any fish, so we caught a little barrel."

That was all he would say. Each time he said it, he added simply:

"It was jolly good."

"But what was in it?" they asked him crossly.

"Oh, I don't know. It was jolly good."

By now the whole of Coqueville was bursting with curiosity. They all stuck their noses into the boat and sniffed hard. There was unanimous agreement that it was a liqueur of some sort but nobody could guess what liqueur. The Emperor, who flattered himself that he had drunk everything that a man can drink, said that he was going to see. Solemnly he took in the hollow of his hand a little of the liquid floating in the bottom of the boat. The crowd fell suddenly silent and waited expectantly. However, after taking a sip, the Emperor shook his head uncertainly, as if still in doubt. He tasted it twice again, with a surprised and worried look on his face, more and more embarrassed. Eventually he was forced to admit:

"I don't know... It's queer. I expect I'd be able to say if it wasn't for the seawater. But my word, it really is very queer."

People looked at each other in amazement that even the Emperor didn't dare to pass a definite judgement on what it was. Coqueville eyed the little cask with respect.

"It was jolly good," said Delphin once again. He seemed to be laughing up his sleeve.

Then, with a broad grin and a wave of his hand, he added:

"If you want some, there's still some left... I saw lots of little barrels... little... little barrels..."

He kept on humming the words like a refrain from some lullaby, looking fondly at Margot, whom he had only just caught sight of. She lifted her hand angrily but he did not blink an eyelid and waited for the slap with a tender look in his eyes.

Intrigued by the thought of this mysterious, delicious drink, Father Radiguet also dipped his finger into the bottom of the boat and sucked it. Like the Emperor, he too shook his head uncertainly: no, he couldn't place it, it was most surprising. One thing only they all agreed on: the cask must have come from the vessel in distress which they had noticed on Sunday and which must have been wrecked. English ships often carried cargoes of liqueurs and fine wines of that sort to Grandport.

The light was slowly fading and the villagers at last started to make their way home in the dark. Only La Queue stayed behind, sunk in thought, turning over in his mind an idea that he wanted to keep to himself. He stopped and listened for the last time to Delphin who was being carried away, still gently singing:

"Little barrels... little barrels... if you want some, there are still some left!"

3

THAT NIGHT the weather changed completely. When Coqueville woke up next day, the sun was shining brightly, the sea was as calm as a millpond, spread out like a piece of green satin. And it was warm, a golden autumnal warmth.

La Queue was first out of bed in the village, his mind still in confusion from last night's dreams. He stood for a long time looking out to sea, to left and right. Finally, he said irritably that he supposed that they'd better keep Monsieur Mouchel satisfied and immediately set out with Tupain and Brisemotte, threatening Margot that he would tickle her ribs if she didn't watch her step. As *Zephyr* was leaving harbour and he saw the *Whale* riding heavily up and down at her moorings, he cheered up somewhat and shouted:

"Well, anyway there'll be nothing doing from them today... Blow out the candle, lads, that drowsy lot are all in bed!"

As soon as he was out at sea, La Queue set his nets, after which he went to look at his pots, that is his long wicker lobster pots, in which you can occasionally catch red mullet as well. But despite the calm sea, his search went unrewarded; all the pots were empty except the last one in which, as if to rub salt into the wound, they found one tiny mackerel which he angrily flung back into the sea. That was the way it went: sometimes weeks would pass and the fish would give Coqueville a miss, and it always happened when Monsieur Mouchel was keen to buy. When La Queue pulled his nets up an hour later, the only thing he had caught was a bunch of seaweed. He clenched his fists and swore; it was all the more irritating because the Atlantic was unbelievably calm and was lying lazily stretched out, drowsing under a blue sky like a sheet of burnished silver, on which *Zephyr* slid slowly and gently along on an even keel. La Queue decided that he would make for harbour after he had dropped his nets once more. He would return and have another look in the afternoon, and he threatened God and all his saints in outrageously blasphemous terms.

Meanwhile Rouget, Fouasse and Delphin were still sound asleep and did not rouse themselves until lunchtime. They could not remember anything except that they were vaguely aware of having enjoyed an amazing treat such as they had never known before. That afternoon, when they were down at the harbour, the Emperor tried to question the three of them, now that they had regained full use of their faculties. Perhaps it was something like a sort of brandy mixed with liquorice juice? Or could it be better described as a kind of sweet rum, with a burnt flavour? First they said yes, then they said no. The Emperor half suspected it might be ratafia* but he couldn't swear to it. Rouget and his crew were too exhausted to go fishing, especially as they knew that La Queue had gone out unsuccessfully that morning; so they were thinking of waiting until the following day before going to look at their pots. They sat with parched throats slumped on blocks of stone, gazing at the incoming tide and barely able to keep awake. Then suddenly Delphin sat up, sprang on to the block of stone and, looking far out to sea, shouted:

"Look over there, guv'nor!"

"What is it?" asked Rouget, stretching himself.

"A barrel."

Their eyes lit up as the other two sprang to their feet and scanned the horizon.

"Where is it, lad? Where is the barrel?" asked Rouget excitedly.

"See that black dot over there, on the left?"

The others could not see anything. Then Rouget uttered an oath:

"Christ Almighty!"

He had just caught sight of the barrel, no bigger than a lentil, against the pale sea, caught in the slanting rays of the setting sun. He ran down to the *Whale* with Delphin and Fouasse sprinting after him like startled rabbits, scattering showers of pebbles as they ran.

As the *Whale* was clearing the harbour mouth, the news of the sighting of the barrel spread like wildfire and the women and children rushed down to the beach. People were shouting:

"A barrel, a barrel!"

"Can you see it? The current's carrying it towards Grandport!"

"Hurry up! That's it, on the left. A barrel!"

And Coqueville streamed down on to the beach, with the children turning cartwheels and the women holding up their skirts with both hands so as to scramble down more quickly. Very soon the whole village was assembled on the beach, just as the evening before.

Margot appeared briefly and then ran back home as fast as she could to warn her father, who was discussing a summons with the Emperor. In the end La Queue came out livid with rage and said to the gamekeeper:

"Stop bothering me! Rouget must've sent you along to waste my time. Well, he's not going to get that one, you'll see!"

When he saw the crew of the *Whale* already three hundred yards off shore rowing madly towards the black dot bobbing up and down in the distance, he became even more enraged.

"No, they're not going to get it! Over my dead body!"

And now Coqueville saw a splendid sight, a wild race between *Zephyr* and the *Whale*. When the crew of the latter saw the other boat leaving harbour, realizing the danger, they redoubled their efforts. Although they had a start of some four hundred yards, it was still an even contest, because *Zephyr* was far lighter and faster. Excitement on the beach was rising to fever pitch. The Mahés and the Floches had instinctively formed into two groups and were following the changing fortunes of the race with passionate interest, each cheering its own boat on. At first the *Whale* held on to its lead but once *Zephyr* was properly underway, she could be seen to be steadily overhauling the other boat. The *Whale* put in a final spurt and for a few minutes managed to hold her advantage, only to be overhauled again as *Zephyr* came up on her at tremendous speed. From that moment onwards, it became apparent that the two boats would reach the barrel roughly together. Victory would depend on circumstances and the slightest error of judgement would determine the issue.

"The *Whale*, the *Whale*!" the Mahés were yelling.

The words froze on their lips. Just as the *Whale* was almost touching the barrel, *Zephyr* boldly slipped in between and pushed the barrel away to the portside, where La Queue harpooned it with a boathook.

"*Zephyr! Zephyr!*" howled the Floches.

And as the Emperor muttered something about "foul play" under his breath, a few rough words were exchanged. Margot was clapping her hands. Father Radiguet, who had come down to the beach holding his breviary, uttered a profound remark which suddenly dowsed everyone's excitement and filled them all with alarm.

"Perhaps they're going to drink the lot, too," he muttered sadly.

Out at sea a violent squabble had arisen between the *Whale* and *Zephyr*. Rouget was accusing La Queue of being a thief while the latter replied by calling Rouget a ne'er-do-well. The two men even picked up their oars to knock each other on the head and the race showed signs of turning into a naval battle. As it was, shaking their fists at each other, they promised to settle the matter ashore, threatening to slit each other's throats as soon as they were on land.

"What a shyster," grunted Rouget. "You know, that cask was bigger than the one yesterday... It's yellow, too. It must be something special."

Then, in a resigned voice:

"Let's go and look at the pots. Perhaps there'll be some lobsters."

And the *Whale* moved ponderously away to the point on the left.

On board *Zephyr*, La Queue had been obliged to speak sharply to Tupain and Brisemotte on the subject of the barrel, for the boathook had loosened one of the hoops and a red liquid was oozing out; the two young men took some of it on the tip of their finger and licked: it was delicious. Surely there wouldn't be any harm in trying just a glass of it? But La Queue put his foot down; he stowed the barrel away and said that the first person to try and have another lick would hear from him. Once ashore, they'd see.

"Shall we go and have a look at the pots, then?" asked Tupain sulkily.

"Yes, in a minute," replied La Queue. "There's no hurry."

He too had been casting fond glances at the cask and in a sudden fit of listlessness, he felt tempted to return to harbour straight away to see what its contents tasted like. He was bored with fish.

"All right," he said after a pause. "Let's get back, it's getting late. We'll look at the pots tomorrow."

But just as he was giving up any idea of fishing, he caught sight of another barrel to starboard, a very tiny cask which was floating upright and spinning like a top. That was the end of any thoughts of fishing nets or lobster pots; they weren't mentioned again. *Zephyr* set off in pursuit of the cask which he picked up quite easily this time.

Meanwhile the *Whale* was engaged in a similar venture. When Rouget had already pulled up five completely empty lobster pots, Delphin, still on the lookout, shouted that he could see something. But it didn't look like a barrel, it was too long.

"It's a piece of wood," said Fouasse.

Rouget let his sixth lobster pot slide back into the sea without bothering to pull it completely out of the water.

"Let's go and have a look all the same," he said.

As they approached, it seemed to them like a plank, a crate or a tree trunk. Then they gave a cry of joy. It was a real barrel but a very queer one, a sort they had never seen before. It looked like a tube bulging in the middle with both ends closed by a layer of plaster.

"Isn't it strange!" exclaimed Rouget delightedly. "I want the Emperor to taste this one... Come on, you two, let's get back!"

They agreed not to broach the barrel straight away and the *Whale* returned to harbour just as *Zephyr* was tying up. The villagers were all still waiting expectantly on the beach. Cheers greeted this unhoped-for catch of three barrels. The young boys flung their caps into the air while the women scurried off to fetch some glasses. They immediately decided to sample the drinks on the spot. Any flotsam and jetsam belonged to the whole community, there was no disputing that! However, they gathered in two groups, the Mahés with Rouget, while the Floches formed a circle round La Queue.

"The first glass is for the Emperor!" cried Rouget. "Tell us what it is!"

The liqueur was a lovely golden yellow. The gamekeeper raised his glass, looked at it, sniffed it and decided to take a sip.

"It's from Holland," he announced after a long pause.

He offered no further information, and the Mahés all drank with due deference. It was slightly viscous and they were surprised by the flowery taste. The women thought it was very good; the men would have preferred a little less sugar. However, in the end, after a third or fourth glass, it did seem quite strong. The more they drank, the better they liked it. The men were becoming merry and the women felt a bit funny.

Meanwhile, despite his recent exchange of words with the mayor, the Emperor was now hanging round the Floche group. The larger barrel contained a dark-red liqueur, while the tiny cask held a liquid as clear as a mountain stream, and it was this last that was the deadliest of them, really peppery and strong enough to take the skin off the roof of your mouth. None of the Floches was able to place either the red or the clear one. Yet some of them were fairly expert and were annoyed not to know the name of the liqueurs that they were drinking with such enjoyment.

"Here you are, Emperor, see what you think of this," La Queue called out at last, making the first move.

The Emperor, who had been hoping for such an invitation, once again assumed his role as taster-in-chief. Having tried the red one, he said:

"There's some orange in it."

For the clear one, he merely said:

"That's a real beauty!"

That was all they could get out of him, because all he did was to keep nodding his head with a knowing look and a pleased expression on his face, like a man who has just done a good job.

Father Radiguet alone seemed unconvinced. He wanted to put a name to them and since, according to him, he had the names on the tip of his tongue, in order to complete his information he kept emptying one glass after another, repeating as he did so:

"Now, wait a second, I know what it is… I'll be able to tell you in a minute."

Meanwhile, everyone was becoming merry, the Mahés as well as the Floches. The latter were laughing particularly loudly because they were mixing their drinks and this made them all the merrier. Both groups were, however, keeping strictly to themselves and not offering any drinks to the other, although they were casting friendly glances at one another, but they were ashamed to admit openly that they would like to try the other group's drink, which was surely better than their own. Despite their rivalry, the two brothers Tupain and Fouasse spent the whole evening in close proximity to one another without once showing signs of wanting to square up to each other. It was noticed, too, that Rouget and his wife were drinking out of the same glass. As for Margot, she was serving drinks to the Floches and as she kept filling the glasses too full, the surplus spilt on to her fingers which she was continually licking, so that, although obeying her father's orders not to drink, she had become tipsy, like the girls during the grape harvest. It was not unbecoming; on the contrary, she was looking all pink and her eyes were sparkling like candles.

The sun was setting; the evening was soft and springlike. Coqueville had demolished the contents of all three barrels and no one was thinking of going home to supper; they were too comfortable on the beach. When it was quite dark, Margot, sitting some distance away from the others, felt someone breathing down the back of her neck: it was Delphin, very merry, crawling on all fours and prowling round her like a wolf. She stifled a cry in order not to draw her father's attention, for he would certainly have booted his behind.

"Do go away, stupid!" she muttered, half laughing and half annoyed, "You'll get caught!"

4

NEXT DAY, when Coqueville awoke, the sun was already high in the heavens. It was an even warmer day and the sea lay stretched out sleepily under a cloudless sky. It was one of those lazy sorts of day when it's wonderful not to have to do anything. It was Wednesday and until lunchtime Coqueville was recovering from its indulgence of the previous evening. Then everyone went down to the beach to take a look.

Fish, Madame Dufeu, Monsieur Mouchel and everything connected with them were forgotten. La Queue didn't even mention going to look at their lobster pots. At about three o'clock they sighted some barrels, four of them, bobbing up and down in front of the village. *Zephyr* and the *Whale* set off in pursuit but as there was enough for all, they didn't squabble and each boat took its share.

At six o'clock, after exploring the bay, Rouget and La Queue came back with three barrels each. And once more, they went on the spree. The women had brought tables down to the beach to make things more comfortable. They even fetched benches and set up two open-air cafés, just like those in Grandport. The Mahés sat on the left, the Floches on the right, separated from each other by a mound of sand. However, that evening the Emperor kept going from one group to the other, carrying round glassfuls of each liqueur, so that everybody could taste the contents of each of the six barrels. By about nine o'clock, everyone was much merrier than on the previous evening. And next morning, no one in Coqueville could ever remember how they had managed to get to bed.

On Thursday, *Zephyr* and the *Whale* picked up only two barrels; that is, two barrels each: but they were enormous. On Friday, the catch was superb, and beyond their wildest dreams: seven barrels, three for Rouget and four for La Queue. And now for Coqueville there began the Golden Age. Nobody did a stroke of work. The fishermen slept off the effects of the night before and did not wake till noon. Then they would go down for a stroll along the beach and look longingly out to sea. Their only concern was which liqueur would come in on the tide. They would sit there for hours, gazing out to sea, and a cry of joy would go up as soon as a barrel hove into view. From the top of the rock, the women and children would wave their arms about wildly at the sight of the tiniest clump of seaweed bobbing up and down in the waves. *Zephyr* and the *Whale* held themselves in readiness to leave at a moment's notice. They sailed out and scoured the bay, fishing for barrels in the same way that people fish for tunny, spurning the carefree mackerel which disported themselves in the sun and the soles floating idly at the surface. Coqueville followed their expeditions from the beach, chuckling with delight. Then, when evening came, they drank their catch.

What really attracted Coqueville's fancy was that the barrels were never-ending. Whenever there seemed to be none left, still they came. The lost ship must have had a wonderful cargo on board and Coqueville, which had become cheerfully selfish, joked about the wrecked vessel: it must have been a proper liqueur cellar, large enough to make every fish in the Atlantic tipsy! What is more, they never caught two identical barrels, for they were of every size, shape and colour, and in every barrel there was a different liqueur, so that the Emperor was in a permanent haze. He had drunk everything that was going and now he was all at sea! La Queue declared that he had never seen such a cargo in his whole life. Father Radiguet expressed the view that it must have been ordered by some native king wanting to set up a cellar. As a matter of fact, Coqueville was so drowsy and fuddled by drinking so many unknown liqueurs that it had given up any attempt to understand.

The ladies preferred the cordials: moka, cacao, peppermint and vanilla. One evening, Marie Rouget drank so much anisette that she was ill. Margot and the other girls went for curaçao, bénédictine, trappistine and chartreuse. The blackcurrant syrup was reserved for the children. The men, of course, enjoyed it most when they had picked up brandies, rums and Holland gins, the sort of stuff that stings the palate. And then there were the surprise items. A cask of resinated raki from Chios threw Coqueville into a state of complete bewilderment;

they thought that they'd come across a barrel of turpentine; all the same, they drank it up, because it's a shame to waste anything, but they talked about it long afterwards. Arak from Batavia, caraway seed schnapps from Sweden, tuica calugaresca from Romania and Serbian slivovitz* also threw Coqueville's ideas on what you can pour down your throat into utter confusion. Basically, they betrayed a weakness for kümmel and kirsch, the sort of spirits that are as clear as crystal and powerful enough to fell an ox. How was it possible for such wonderful drinks to have been invented? Up till now, Coqueville had had experience of only the rawest of spirits, and not everyone had known them. And so their imagination began to run riot and they felt like going down on their knees to worship such an inexhaustible variety of intoxicating liquor. Fancy being able to get drunk every day on something new that you didn't even know the name of! It was like a fairy story, a shower of nectar, a fountain spurting with every sort of extraordinary liquid, distillations scented with the fruits and flowers of the whole of creation!

And so on Friday evening, there were seven barrels set up on the beach and the whole of Coqueville was there as well; indeed, the villagers were there all the time for, thanks to the mild weather, they were all living on the beach. Never had they known such a gorgeous week in September. They had been on the spree since Monday and there was no reason for it not to last for ever if divine Providence continued its supply of barrels. Father Radiguet saw the hand of God in all this. All business was suspended; why toil and sweat when pleasure was handed to you, in a bottle, while you slept? They had all become members of the leisured classes, people who were in a position to drink expensive liqueurs without having to worry who was footing the bill. With their hands in their pockets, the inhabitants of Coqueville lounged about in the sun awaiting their evening treat. As a matter of fact, they were never sober; kümmel, kirsch and ratafia were the links in an unbroken chain of jollification. In the space of seven days, Coqueville was being inflamed by gin, made sentimental by curaçao and hilarious by brandy. And they were as innocent and as ignorant as babes in arms, drinking everything the good Lord provided with the simple faith of true believers.

It was on Friday that the Mahés and the Floches started fraternizing. Everyone was very merry that evening. The barriers between them had already begun to crumble the previous day, when some of the tipsiest among them had kicked away the mound of sand separating the two groups. There was only one further step needed. The Floches were busily emptying their four barrels while the Mahés were similarly engaged in finishing off their three small casks, which happened to contain liqueurs of the same colours as the French flag, red, white, and blue. The Floches were very envious of the blue one because a blue liqueur seemed to them something quite out of the ordinary. Now that he was never sober, La Queue had become extremely genial and he suddenly went across unsteadily, with a glass in his hand, realizing that as mayor, it was up to him to make the first move.

"Look, Rouget," he said, stumbling somewhat over his words, "would you care to have a drink with me?"

"I don't mind if I do," replied Rouget, swaying with emotion.

And they fell on each other's necks. At this touching sight, everyone burst into tears and the Mahés and the Floches embraced each other after being at daggers drawn for three centuries. Father Radiguet, greatly stirred, again spoke of the hand of God. They drank each other's health in the three liqueurs, red, white and blue.

"*Vive la France!*" the Emperor cried.

The blue one was no good at all, the white one just passable, but the red one was terrific. After that, they set about the Floches' barrels. Then they started dancing. As there was no band, some of the young men obliged by whistling and clapping their hands. This set the girls going. It was a proper binge. The seven barrels were all placed in one long line and everyone could choose the one he liked best. Those who had had enough lay down on the sand and had a nap; when they woke up, they started again. The dancers gradually spread out until there was dancing all over the beach. This open-air hop went on till midnight. The sea lapped gently and the stars shone brightly in the calm of the fathomless depths of the heavens. It was like some primitive tribe, in the infancy of the world, peacefully cradled in the joyous intoxication of their first barrel of brandy.

However, Coqueville still went home when it was time to go to bed. When there was nothing left to drink, the Mahés and the Floches, supporting and carrying each other as best they could, eventually made their way back to their houses. On Saturday, the celebration went on until nearly two o'clock in the morning. During the day, they had caught six barrels, two of which were enormous. Fouasse and Tupain nearly came to blows and Tupain, who became aggressive when drunk, threatened to do his brother in. But everyone was disgusted at such an exhibition, the Floches as well as the Mahés. Was it sensible to go on squabbling like that when the whole village was overflowing with brotherly love? So they forced the two brothers to drink each other's health, which they reluctantly did. The Emperor promised himself to keep an eye on them. The Rouget couple were not very happy either. When Marie had been drinking anisette, she allowed Brisemotte to take liberties that were not to her husband's liking, all the more so as drink had made him also amorously inclined. Father Radiguet had tried to pour oil on troubled waters by preaching the forgiveness of sins, but everyone was apprehensive at the possibility of an outburst.

"Ah well," said La Queue, "things will sort themselves out. If there's a good catch tomorrow, you'll see... Your very good health!"

However, La Queue himself was not entirely guiltless. He was still keeping a sharp eye on Delphin and trying to kick his backside every time he saw him sidling up to Margot. The Emperor indignantly pointed out that there was no sense in trying to prevent two young folk from having fun but La Queue still swore that he'd see his daughter dead rather than let Delphin have her. Anyway, Margot didn't want him.

"That's right, isn't it?" he shouted. "You're too proud ever to marry a tramp, aren't you?"

"No, I never would, Papa!" Margot invariably replied.

On Saturday, Margot drank a good deal of a very sweet liqueur. You can't imagine how sweet it was. As Margot was quite unsuspecting, she soon found herself sitting on the ground beside the barrel. She was laughing happily to herself: it was heavenly, she could see stars and hear dance tunes singing in her ears. Then it was that Delphin slid up to her under the cover of the barrel and took her hand.

"Will you, Margot?" he asked her.

"It's Papa who doesn't want me to," she replied, still smiling.

"Oh, that doesn't matter," retorted the boy. "Old people never do, you know... As long as you want to..."

And he boldly planted a kiss on her neck. She squirmed with pleasure and little shivers ran down her back.

"Stop it, you're tickling..."

But she made no mention of giving him a slap. For one thing, she couldn't have done it, because her hands had gone all weak, while for another, she was finding those little kisses on her neck rather nice. It was like the liqueur which was filling her with a delicious feeling of languor. After a while, she twisted her head and stretched out her chin, like a cat.

"Look," she said in a voice that trembled, "I'm itching just there, under my ear… Oh, that's wonderful…"

They had both forgotten La Queue. Fortunately the Emperor was on the alert. He drew Father Radiguet's attention to them.

"Look over there, Father. They'd better get married."

"Morality would certainly suggest so," observed the priest sententiously.

And he promised to see what he could do about arranging it next day: he would personally have a word with La Queue. Meanwhile La Queue himself had drunk so much that the Emperor and the priest had to carry him home. On the way, they tried to make him see reason with regard to Delphin and his daughter, but all they could get out of him was grunts. Delphin followed behind them, taking Margot home under the bright starry sky.

Next day, *Zephyr* and the *Whale* had already picked up seven barrels by four o'clock. At six o'clock they caught two more. That made nine in all. And so Coqueville celebrated the Sabbath day. It was the seventh day of inebriation and it was a celebration to end all celebrations, a beano such as no one had ever seen before nor would ever see again. Mention this to anyone from Lower Normandy and they'll chuckle and say:

"Ah yes, what a binge they had in Coqueville!"

5

M EANWHILE, even as early as Tuesday, Monsieur Mouchel had expressed surprise at seeing neither Rouget nor La Queue. What the devil were they up to? The sea was calm, they should have made a splendid catch. Perhaps they were waiting in the hope of getting a big haul of lobsters and sole which they could bring over all together. So he decided to be patient and see what happened on Wednesday.

But on Wednesday, Monsieur Mouchel got cross. It must be remembered that Dufeu's widow was an awkward customer; it did not take long for her to become abusive. So although he was a fine, upstanding young fellow, well-built, with a mop of fair hair, she made him quake in his shoes, despite his secret dreams of one day making her his wife; he was thus always careful to show her every attention while reserving the right to bring her to heel with a good slap round the face if he ever became the boss. Well, that Wednesday morning, the widow raged and swore, complaining that no fish was being delivered and putting the blame on him for gadding about with the local girls instead of concentrating on whiting and mackerel, of which there should have been a plentiful supply. Thus provoked, Monsieur Mouchel declared that it was Coqueville's fault for not having kept their word. For a brief moment, Madame Dufeu's surprise at the news of such strange behaviour made her forget her anger. What on earth was Coqueville thinking of? They'd never done that sort of thing before. But she hastened to add that she didn't give a damn about Coqueville, that it was Monsieur Mouchel's responsibility and if he kept on being taken in by the fishermen, she'd have to decide what measures to take. This remark made the young man very uneasy and he consigned Rouget and La Queue to the bottomless pit. But perhaps they'd come next day.

Next day was Thursday and still neither of them put in an appearance. In the late afternoon, a despairing Monsieur Mouchel climbed up to the rock to the left of Grandport, where he had a view of Coqueville in the distance, together with its yellow strip of beach. He stayed looking for a long time. It seemed peaceful enough under the sun. Wisps of smoke were coming out of the chimneys: no doubt wives were getting the supper ready. Monsieur Mouchel saw that Coqueville was still there and that it hadn't been crushed by a fall of rock. He was more mystified than ever. Just as he was about to go down, he thought he could see two dark spots in the bay, the *Whale* and *Zephyr*. He went back and reassured the widow: Coqueville was out fishing.

Night came and went; it was Friday and still no trace of Coqueville. Monsieur Mouchel climbed a dozen times up to the rock. He was beginning to lose his nerve; Madame Dufeu was treating him abominably and he could think of no possible explanation to give her. Coqueville was still there, lazily basking in the sun like a lizard. But this time Monsieur Mouchel could not see any smoke. The village seemed dead. Had they all crawled into their holes and given up the ghost? Certainly, the beach seemed to be swarming with people but that could well be heaps of seaweed brought in by the tide.

On Saturday, still nobody appeared. The widow had stopped shouting and was sitting there tight-lipped and with eyes set hard. Monsieur Mouchel spent two hours up on his rock. He was becoming curious and beginning to feel that he must discover for himself why the village seemed so deserted.

Finally, the sight of those tumbledown old cottages blissfully drowsing in the sun irritated him so much that he resolved to leave very early on Monday, so as to be there by nine o'clock in the morning.

Getting to Coqueville was no easy matter. Monsieur Mouchel decided to go by land, so that he could descend on the village unawares. He drove in a horse and cart as far as Robigneux, where he left them in a barn, since it would have been foolhardy to risk driving down the gullies. He set off at a steady pace for Coqueville, a distance of more than four miles over the roughest of tracks. The road, in fact, runs through a wild and picturesque landscape, twisting and turning as it descends between two enormous sloping walls of rock, so narrow in parts that three men could not walk abreast. Further on, it ran along a sheer drop, until the gorge suddenly opened out to give views over the immense blue horizon and the sea. But Monsieur Mouchel was in no mood to admire the landscape and he swore as the boulders rolled away under his feet. It was all Coqueville's fault and he promised to show them the rough edge of his tongue when he arrived. He was now nearly there and as he came round the last bend in the rock he caught sight of the twenty or so houses which comprised the village, huddled together against the cliff-face.

It was just striking nine. The sky was blue and it was so warm that you could have thought it was June. The air was clear and there was a golden glow and a cool salty smell of sea. Monsieur Mouchel set off down the only street of the village, which he had often visited, and as he had to pass Rouget's house, he went in. The house was empty. Then, he had a brief look into Tupain's, Fouasse's and Brisemotte's cottages. Not a soul to be seen; the doors were all open but the rooms were empty. What could it mean? A cold shiver began to run down his spine. Then he thought of the local authorities: the Emperor would certainly be able to give him information. But the Emperor's house was as empty as all the rest – so even the gamekeeper wasn't there! By now, the silence of the deserted village filled him with terror. He hurried on to the mayor's house where another surprise awaited him. The inside of the house was in a frightful mess: beds left unmade for the last three days, dirty crockery lying about all over the place, chairs tipped up as if there had been a fight. Now completely unnerved and with thoughts of some dreadful cataclysm running through his mind, Monsieur Mouchel made for the church, determined to leave no stone unturned, but the priest was no more visible than the mayor. Religion had vanished together with any civil authority.

Coqueville had been abandoned and left with not a breath of life, not even a dog or a cat. And not even poultry, for the hens had left as well. Absolutely nothing at all: empty and silent, Coqueville lay plunged in slumber beneath the vast blue sky.

Heavens above! It wasn't surprising if Coqueville wasn't supplying any fish! Coqueville had moved out, Coqueville was dead! The police must be informed. Monsieur Mouchel was deeply moved by this mysterious disaster, but then, thinking that he might as well go down as far as the beach, he uttered a sudden cry. There, flat out on the sand, lay the entire population. He thought at first that there must have been a general massacre, but the sound of heavy snoring quickly disabused him. On Sunday night, Coqueville had celebrated until such a late hour that its inhabitants had been quite incapable of going home to bed. So they had slept on the beach, in the place where they had toppled over around the nine barrels of liqueur, now completely empty.

Yes, the whole of Coqueville lay there plunged in sleep, and I mean by that the women and children and old men, as well as the working men. There was not one still on his feet. Some were lying face down, some on their backs, others lay curled up. As you make your bed, so you must lie on it. And so the whole lot were scattered all over the beach where their drunkenness had landed them, like a handful of leaves blown at random by the wind. Some of the men had tipped over with their heads hanging down while some of the women were showing their backsides. It was all free and easy, a dormitory in the open air, good honest folk and not a trace of embarrassment, because embarrassment is the enemy of enjoyment. There happened to be a new moon and so, thinking that they had blown out their candles, the inhabitants of Coqueville had let themselves go. Day had come and the sun was shining brightly, straight into the sleepers' eyes, but not one eye blinked. They were all sleeping like logs and beaming all over their faces with that wonderful innocence of the drunk. The hens, too, must have come down early to peck at the barrels, because they too were lying on the sand, dead drunk. There were even five cats and three dogs, flat on their backs with their paws in the air, tipsy from licking the sugary dregs left in the glasses.

Monsieur Mouchel picked his way through the sleepers for a while, taking care not to disturb anyone. He realized what had happened because they had picked up some casks from the wrecked English vessel in Grandport. His anger had completely evaporated. What a touching sight it was! Coqueville was reconciled and the Mahés were lying down with the Floches... When the last glass had been drained, the worst enemies had fallen into each other's arms: Tupain and Fouasse were snoring away hand in hand, like brothers who henceforth would find it impossible to quarrel over legacies. As for the Rougets, they offered an even more charming picture: Marie lay sleeping between Rouget and Brisemotte, as though saying that from now on they would live happily like that, for ever afterwards...

But there was one group that provided a particularly touching family scene: Delphin and Margot were lying with their arms round each other's necks, cheek to cheek, with their lips still open in a kiss, while the Emperor was lying crosswise at their feet, keeping guard over them; La Queue was sound asleep and snoring away like any happy father who had found a husband for his daughter, and Father Radiguet, who had toppled over like all the rest, was holding his arms outspread as though blessing them. In sleep, Margot was still holding up her pretty little face like the muzzle of a lovesick cat who enjoys being tickled under its chin.

So the spree ended in a wedding. And later on, Monsieur Mouchel himself married the widow and tanned her hide as he had promised.

Mention all this to anyone from Lower Normandy and they'll chuckle and say:

"Ah yes, what a binge they had in Coqueville!"

Dead Men Tell No Tales[*]

1

I DIED ON A SATURDAY MORNING AT SIX A.M., after an illness lasting three days. My poor wife was rummaging in a trunk for some bed linen. When she stood up and saw me stretched out, all stiff, with my eyes open, not breathing, she rushed over to my bedside, thinking that I had fainted. She felt my hands and bent over to look into my face. Then, horror-struck, she burst into tears and stammered distractedly:

"Dear God! Dear God! He's dead!"

I could hear everything but the sounds were muffled and seemed to be coming from a great distance. My left eye was still capable of perceiving a vague gleam, a milky sort of light in which objects were melting into one another, but my right eye was completely paralysed. My whole being was in a sort of syncope, as if I had been struck by lightning. I was reduced to a state of complete inertia; not one muscle of my body would obey me. And in this state of numbness, all that remained was an ability to think, sluggishly but still with complete clarity.

My poor Marguerite had fallen on her knees beside my bed and she was sobbing in a heart-rending voice:

"Dear God! He's dead! He's dead!"

Could this strange state of torpor be death? This complete physical impotence which still left my intelligence capable of functioning? Was it my soul still lingering on inside my skull before it took flight for ever? I had been subject to fits since earliest childhood and had almost succumbed to bouts of fever on two occasions, when still quite young. After that, those around me had become used to my chronic bad health, and when I had had to take to my bed in our room in the furnished hotel in the Rue Dauphine[*] the day after our arrival in Paris, I myself had dissuaded Marguerite from sending for a doctor. I thought all I needed was a little rest; I was merely tired out after the journey. Nevertheless, I was in a dreadfully agitated state of mind.

63

We had come up from our home in the country at extremely short notice, almost penniless, with barely enough money to see us through to my first month's salary in the government office job to which I had just been appointed. And now I had died from this unexpected attack of fever.

Could this really be death? I'd always imagined that it would be so much darker, so much quieter than this. Even as a lad I had been afraid of dying. Being a sickly child, people would stroke my hand with pity in their eyes. I always had the feeling that I would not live long, that I was going to an early grave. And the idea of being buried filled me with a dread that I could never come to terms with, despite the fact that it never left me, night or day, and as I grew up, this idea became an obsession. Sometimes, after thinking about it for days, I would imagine that I had succeeded in conquering my fear. All right, you'll die and that will be the end of you, everyone has to die some day, there could be nothing more normal and proper. I would almost manage to be cheerful about it: I could look death in the face without flinching! And then, quite suddenly, an icy shiver would run down my spine and I would become sick with fear, as if some giant hand were holding me suspended over a precipice. My terror at the thought of being buried would flood back and all my fine reasoning would be swept away. How often would I wake up in the night with a sudden start, not knowing what unseen spirit had chilled me with its icy breath, and I would clasp my hands and stammer: "Oh God, oh God, we all have to die!" My chest would contract with fear and the inevitability of death seemed all the more horrible in the confusion of my sudden awakening. And I was so unnerved that I hardly dared to go to sleep again, for sleep was so akin to death. Suppose I were to go to sleep for ever, close my eyes and never open them again?

I don't know if others suffer in this way but my life has been wrecked by such fears. Death has always stood between me and everything I loved. I can recall my happiest moments with Marguerite, the first few months of our marriage when she would be sleeping beside me and I would be thinking of her and making plans for our future, and my feeling of joy would constantly be destroyed by the presentiment that we must inevitably be torn apart; so all my hopes were poisoned and I would be thrown into a deep depression. What was the point of our present happiness if we were fated to be separated? My morbid imagination gloated over the idea of bereavement: which of us would go first? And the thought of either alternative filled my eyes with tears as the picture of our broken lives unrolled before me. Even during the happiest periods of my life such thoughts would overcome me and no one could understand my sudden fits of sadness. When some good luck came my way, people were amazed to see me looking so gloomy; it was because the thought of my utter extinction had suddenly crossed my mind. The terrible question: "What's the use?" kept ringing in my ears like a death knell. But the greatest torment of all is to have to keep all such thoughts to yourself, as a shameful secret, a sickness that you can never admit to anyone. Often a husband and wife lying in bed, side by side, must feel the same cold shiver of horror run through them; yet neither of them will say a word, because you don't talk about death any more than you utter certain obscene expressions. You're so afraid of death that you dare not mention it; you keep it hidden in the same way as you hide your genitals.

All these thoughts were running through my mind as Marguerite continued desperately sobbing. I felt sorry not to be able to comfort her by telling her that I was in no pain. If death was merely this bodily weakness, then I had indeed been wrong to be in such dread of it. I had a smug feeling of well-being and restfulness that cancelled all my worries. Above all, my memory had become extremely active; my whole life was passing rapidly before my eyes like a spectacle from which I felt completely divorced. It was an odd and amusing experience, as though some distant voice was telling the story of my life.

I was pursued by the memory of a tiny patch of countryside near Guérande, on the road to Piriac. The road makes a bend and a little pinewood sweeps down a rocky slope. I was seven at the time. I used to go there with my father to a little, half-ruined house to eat pancakes with Marguerite's parents, who were even then barely managing to scrape a living working in the local salt marshes. Then I recalled my boarding school at Nantes and its dreary old walls where I grew up longing for the broad horizons of Guérande with its salt marshes stretching as far as the eye could see at the foot of the town and the immense ocean spread out under the sky. Now there came a black hole in my memories; my father died and I got a job as a clerk in the hospital. My monotonous life had begun; the only bright spots were my Sunday visits to the old house on the Piriac road. But there things were going from bad to worse, for the salt marshes were in dire straits and the whole region was being reduced to abject poverty. Marguerite was still only a child. She was fond of me because I pushed her round in a wheelbarrow. But later on, when I asked her to marry me, I realized from her terrified look that she thought me hideously ugly. Her parents gave their consent straight away, to get her off their hands. She was a dutiful daughter and didn't protest. Once she had grown used to the idea of becoming my wife, she no longer seemed quite so unhappy. I remember that on our wedding day, it was raining cats and dogs in Guérande and when we went home she had to strip down to her petticoat because her dress was wet through.

And that was all the youth I ever had. We lived in Guérande for a while and then one day I came home and found her crying her heart out. She was bored and wanted to move. After six months of pinching and scraping and working overtime, I managed to save enough and when a former friend of the family succeeded in finding a job for me, I had taken her with me to Paris, so that the poor girl would be less miserable. In the train she was laughing all the time. When night came, as the third-class seats were so hard, I took her on to my knees so that she could sleep more comfortably.

But all that belonged to the past, and now I had just died and my wife was kneeling, sobbing, on the tiled floor beside the narrow bed of our lodging-house room. The white spot that I could see with my left eye was growing dimmer but I could still remember the room perfectly. The chest of drawers was on the left, the fireplace on the right and on the mantelshelf above there stood a clock which was not working because it had lost its pendulum; its hands pointed to six minutes past ten. The window looked out onto the Rue Dauphine. All the traffic of Paris seemed to be going through that deep, gloomy street, making a din that set the window panes rattling.

We knew not a soul in Paris. As we had left in a hurry, I was not expected to report for work until the following Monday. Ever since I had been forced to take to my bed, I had had the feeling of being imprisoned in this room where we had landed up, bewildered, after our journey, having spent some fifteen hours in the train, and stunned by the bustle in the streets. My wife had looked after me, kind and cheerful as always, but I could sense how worried she was. Every so often, she would go over to the window and glance down into the street, and

66

she would come back looking very pale, scared by the size of Paris where she knew not one brick or stone and which was creating such a deafening roar. And what was she going to do should I never wake up? What would become of her, all alone in this immense metropolis, completely ignorant, and without anyone to support her?

Marguerite had caught hold of one of my hands dangling limply beside the bed and she was kissing it as she repeated:

"Oh Olivier, do say something! Oh God, he's dead, he's dead!"

So death didn't mean complete annihilation, for I could hear her and I was capable of reasoning. It had only been this thought of annihilation that had terrified me ever since I was a child. I could not imagine the total destruction of my whole being, my complete extinction, and it would be for all eternity, century upon century without ever coming to life again! Sometimes when I saw in my newspaper a mention of a date in the next century, a shudder would run through me, for by that time I should certainly not be still alive and that year in a future that I should never see, when I should no longer exist, filled me with terror. Didn't the world exist only for me and wouldn't it collapse when I abandoned it? It had always been my hope to be able to meditate on life once I was dead, but no doubt my present state wasn't death and I should surely be waking up soon. Yes, in a few minutes, I should lean forwards and take Marguerite in my arms and dry her tears. What a joyful reunion that would be! And how much more dearly we should love each other then! I'd rest for a couple of days and then start work. A new life would begin for us both, a happier, richer life. But there was no need to hurry; later on would do, for the moment I was too exhausted. Marguerite was wrong to be so sad merely because I didn't feel strong enough at the moment to turn my head on the pillow and smile up at her. In a very short while, when she next said: "He's dead! Oh God, he's dead!" I'd kiss her and say to her very, very softly, so as not to scare her: "No, my darling, I was just asleep, you can see, I'm alive and I love you."

2

HEARING MARGUERITE'S CRIES, someone pushed open the door and a voice exclaimed:

"What's the matter?... Has he had another attack?"

I recognized the voice: It was Madame Gabin, an old woman who lived next door on the same landing. When we had arrived, she had sympathized with our predicament and had been very obliging. She had also immediately told us all about herself. Last winter, a hard-hearted landlord had sold up all her furniture, since when she had been living in the hotel with her daughter Adèle, a little girl of ten. They both earned a living by cutting out lampshades, which brought them in two francs a day at most.

"Heavens above, is he dead?" she asked, lowering her voice.

I realized that she was coming over to look at me. Then she touched me and said in a pitying voice:

"Oh, you poor girl, you poor girl!"

By now Marguerite was exhausted and sobbing like a child. Madame Gabin helped her to her feet and sat her down in a rickety armchair beside the fireplace, trying to comfort her.

"Come on now, you mustn't take on like that. Just because your husband has passed on, there's no point in thinking it's the end of the world. Of course, when I lost my hubby, I felt just like you, I couldn't swallow a mouthful for three whole days... But that didn't do any good, quite the reverse, it made me feel much worse. Come on now, be sensible, for goodness' sake!"

Marguerite gradually calmed down; she was rapidly becoming exhausted, although every now and then she was shaken by sobs. Meanwhile the gruff old woman was firmly taking charge.

"Now don't you worry, dear," she kept saying. "My little Dédé has just gone off to hand in our work and neighbours must stand by each other, mustn't they?... Well, I can see you haven't finished unpacking yet, but there is some linen in the chest of drawers, isn't there?"

I heard her opening the chest of drawers. She must have taken out a towel that she spread over the bedside table. Next she struck a match, which made me think that she was lighting one of the tallow candles from the mantel shelf, since we hadn't any wax tapers. I was able to follow her every movement about the room and realize everything she was doing.

"Oh, the poor gentleman!" she murmured. "What a good thing it was that I heard you cry out, my dear."

Then suddenly the vague gleam of light that I could still see with my left eye disappeared. Madame Gabin had just closed my eyes. I hadn't felt her fingers touching my eyelids. When I realized what had happened, a slow chill started creeping over my body.

The door now opened again and her little ten-year-old daughter Dédé came in, piping in her shrill voice:

"Mummy, Mummy! Oh, I knew you were here. Here's the money. We got three francs twenty for our lampshades. I took them twenty dozen!"

"Sh, sh! Don't make a noise," her mother said, vainly trying to keep her quiet.

As the little girl still kept on talking, her mother must have pointed to the bed, for she stopped abruptly and I could sense that she was retreating uneasily towards the door.

"Is the gentleman asleep?" she asked in a low voice.

"Yes. Now go away and play," her mother replied.

But the child stayed where she was. She must have been staring at me with a scared look on her face, half realizing what had happened. Suddenly she was seized with a sort of panic and ran out of the room, knocking over a chair.

"Oh Mummy, he's dead!"

Silence fell. Marguerite was sitting exhausted in the armchair; she had stopped crying. Madame Gabin continued to prowl round the room. She was muttering between her teeth:

"You can't keep anything from children these days. Look at her. As God's my witness, I'm bringing her up properly! Whenever she runs an errand or I send her to deliver our lampshades, I work out how long it'll take, to make sure she doesn't go gallivanting about. But it's no use, she knows everything, she saw straight away what had happened, yet she's only ever seen one dead person, her uncle François, and she wasn't quite four at the time... What can you do, children aren't children any more."

She broke off and changed the subject:

"I say, dear, we mustn't forget, there are a lot of formalities, we've got to notify the town hall and make arrangements for the funeral. You're in no fit state to see to all that and I don't want to leave you on your own. What do you say to letting me go and see if Monsieur Simoneau is at home?"

Marguerite made no reply. I felt as if I was witnessing all this from a great distance. Occasionally, it seemed to me that I was floating round in the room like a flickering flame while a stranger, a shapeless mass, was lying inert on the bed. All the same, I should have preferred her not to agree to asking Monsieur Simoneau to help. I'd caught sight of him three or four times during my short illness. He occupied a neighbouring room and had been very obliging. Madame Gabin had told us that he was merely passing through Paris, having come to collect some outstanding debts on behalf of his father, recently deceased after leaving Paris to go and live in the country. Simoneau was a tall, strapping young fellow, very good-looking. I had taken an instant dislike to him, perhaps because he was so healthy. On the previous day, he had once again come in and I had felt unhappy to see him sitting close to Marguerite. She looked so pretty and fresh beside him! And he had looked at her very attentively when she smiled at him and said how kind he was to come and ask after me!

"Here's Monsieur Simoneau," announced Madame Gabin in a hushed voice as she returned.

He pushed the door gently open and as soon as she caught sight of him, Marguerite burst into tears again. The presence of this man, the only friend she had in Paris, had awakened her grief. He made no attempt to comfort her. I could not see him but in the darkness which surrounded me I could picture his face and clearly imagine him looking perturbed and unhappy to see this poor young woman in such despair. And yet she must have looked most appealing with her fair hair all dishevelled, her pale face and her dear little feverish, childlike hands!

"I'll be very glad to do anything you require," Monsieur Simoneau said gently. "I'll take care of everything if you like."

She could only stammer a few words of thanks in reply. But Madame Gabin went out with the young man and I heard her mention the word "money" as she passed close by my bed. Funerals cost a lot of money and she was afraid that the poor young woman was penniless; anyway, they could enquire from her. Simoneau cut the old woman short: he didn't want Marguerite to be bothered; he would go to the town hall and he would see to the arrangements for the funeral.

When silence again fell, I wondered to myself how much longer this nightmare would last. I must be alive because I could understand the slightest things that were taking place around me. I was also beginning to realize exactly the sort of state I was in: it must be a sort of catalepsy, of which I had heard. Even as a child, at the time of my worst nervous troubles, I had suffered similar attacks, lasting several hours. It was obviously one of these that had reduced me to this state of complete immobility, similar to death, which was misleading everyone round me. But my heart would start beating properly again, my blood would start circulating and my muscles would relax. I should wake up and comfort Marguerite. So, with these arguments running through my mind, I urged myself to be patient.

Hours went by. Madame Gabin had fetched her lunch but Marguerite was refusing to eat anything. Through the open window there came the noise from the Rue Dauphine below. A little clink of the copper candlestick against the marble top of the bedside table suggested to me that they were replacing the old candle. At last Simoneau returned.

"Well?" the old woman asked him in a low voice.

"Everything's arranged," he replied. "The funeral will set off from here at eleven o'clock tomorrow morning. You needn't worry about anything and don't talk about all this in front of that poor girl."

Madame Gabin now pointed out that the doctor still had not come to certify death.

Simoneau went over and sat down beside Marguerite, trying at first to comfort her, but he soon fell silent. "The funeral will set off from here at eleven o'clock tomorrow morning." These words were ringing in my ears like a death knell. And there would be the doctor to certify death, in Madame Gabin's words! Surely he would see straight away that I was merely unconscious? I started waiting for his arrival with frantic impatience.

Meanwhile the day dragged on. To avoid wasting her time, Madame Gabin had fetched her lampshades and had even asked if Dédé could join her, saying that she didn't like leaving children too long on their own.

"Come on in," she whispered to the little girl as she ushered her into the room. "And remember, you must behave yourself and not look over there or else there'll be trouble."

She was forbidding her daughter to look at me; it seemed the right thing to do. However, Dédé must certainly have been looking furtively in my direction now and again, because I heard her mother slapping her arm and saying crossly:

"If you don't get on with your work, I'll send you out of the room and tonight that gentleman will come along when you're in bed and pull your feet!"

Both mother and daughter had sat down at our table and I could distinctly hear the sound of their scissors cutting out the lampshades. No doubt this was quite a difficult and complicated operation, for they were not getting on very fast. To fight back my growing anxiety, I started counting the lampshades one by one.

The only sound to be heard in the room was the click of scissors. Overcome by fatigue, Marguerite must have dozed off. Twice Simoneau got to his feet and I was tortured by the thought that he was taking advantage of the fact that Marguerite was asleep to press his lips on her hair and kiss it. I didn't know him but I was sure that he loved my wife. Then suddenly little Dédé laughed. It was the last straw.

"What are you laughing at, you silly girl?" her mother asked her. "I'll send you out onto the landing if you're not careful. Well, what are you laughing at?"

The little girl stammered that she hadn't been laughing but coughing. But I imagined that she must have seen Simoneau bending over Marguerite and that she found that funny.

The lamp had already been lit. There was a knock at the door.

"That'll be the doctor," the old woman said.

It was indeed the doctor. He did not even bother to apologize for being so late. No doubt he had had to climb many flights of stairs in the course of the day. The light was very dim. He asked:

"Is this where the body is?"

"Yes, doctor," replied Simoneau.

Marguerite stood up, trembling. Madame Gabin had sent Dédé out on to the landing, because a child has no business seeing that sort of thing, and she was trying to lead my wife over to the window to spare her the painful spectacle.

Meanwhile, the doctor had quickly made his way towards the bed. I had the feeling that he was tired, impatient and in no mood to linger. Did he take hold of my hand? Did he place his own hand on my heart? I can't say one way or the other, but it seemed to me that he had, quite unconcernedly, been content merely to bend over me.

"Shall I bring the lamp over so that you can see better?" Simoneau offered obligingly.

"No, there's no need," the doctor replied calmly.

No need? This man, who was holding my life in his hands, thought there was no need to make a thorough examination! And yet I wasn't dead!

"At what time did he die?" he went on.

"At six o'clock this morning," replied Simoneau.

A furious protest surged up inside me, despite the terrible weight that was holding me down. Oh, the horror of not being able to say a word or stir a single limb!

The doctor added:

"This sultry weather is dreadful. There's nothing so exhausting as this early spring weather."

And he moved away from the bed and, with him, all my chances of survival. Shouts and sobs and abuse were struggling convulsively for utterance, stifled for lack of breath. Ah, that miserable doctor, so blinkered in his professional routine that he had become nothing more than a robot who took people's deaths as a mere formality! What a complete idiot the man must be! All his pretended medical science was a sham, since he couldn't distinguish between a dead man and a live one. And now he was leaving me and going away!

"Goodnight, doctor," Simoneau said.

There was silence. The doctor must have been bowing to Marguerite who had come back into the room, while Madame Gabin was closing the window. Then he left and I heard his footsteps going downstairs.

So this was the end. I was doomed: my last hope was vanishing with those footsteps. If I didn't wake up before eleven o'clock tomorrow, I'd be buried alive. And this thought was so terrifying that I lost consciousness of everything around me: it was a swoon as deep as death itself. The last sound I heard was the click of Madame Gabin's and Dédé's scissors. The funeral vigil was beginning. Nobody spoke. Marguerite had refused to go and sleep in her neighbour's room and was reclining in the armchair, pale and beautiful, with her closed lids still wet with tears, while Simoneau sat opposite her, silently watching her in the darkness.

3

I CANNOT BEGIN TO DESCRIBE all that I went through the following morning. It was an anguish that has remained with me like some appalling dream during which I experienced such confused and peculiar feelings that it would be difficult for me to detail them here. And what made my suffering even more intense was that I was still hoping against hope that I would suddenly wake up. But as the time for the funeral approached, my feeling of dread grew more and more oppressive.

It was not until the following morning that I once again became aware of the people and objects surrounding me. As I was dozing, the clatter of a window catch aroused me. It was Madame Gabin letting in some fresh air. It must have been about seven o'clock, for I could hear the cries of street traders, the high-pitched voice of a little girl selling chickweed and a hoarse voice offering carrots for sale. At first this noisy awakening of the Paris streets helped to calm me: it seemed impossible that they would be putting me underground amidst all this activity, and I remembered something else which further reassured me: I recalled that I had seen a similar case to mine when I had been employed in the hospital in Guérande. Like me, a man had remained asleep for twenty-eight hours, a sleep so deep, in fact, that the doctors were hesitating whether they should not declare him dead, and then he had sat up and been able to get out of bed straight away. I myself had already been sleeping for twenty-five hours. If I woke up at about ten o'clock, there would still be time.

I tried to work out who was in the room and what they were doing. Young Dédé must have been playing on the landing, because the door was open and I could hear a child laughing outside. Simoneau had no doubt left: I could detect no sign of his presence. Only Madame Gabin could be heard shuffling round in her slippers. Finally someone spoke:

"Now dear," the old woman said, "you're to drink up while it's still hot, it'll do you good."

She was addressing Marguerite and the gentle drip of a filter on the mantelpiece told me that she was making coffee.

"I must say that I needed that," she went on. "Staying up all night's bad for you at my time of life. And it's so sad in the night, in a place where something dreadful's happened... Now do have some coffee, dear, just a drop."

And she forced Marguerite to take a cup.

"You see? It's warm, it cheers you up. You need to get your strength back for what you've got to go through today. Now if you were really sensible, you'd go to my room and wait there."

"No, I want to stay here," Marguerite replied firmly.

This was the first time I had heard her voice since the previous day and I was deeply moved. It was quite changed, broken with emotion.

Oh, my darling Marguerite! I could feel her close beside me, offering me my last consolation, I knew that her eyes never left my face, and that she was crying broken-heartedly.

But the minutes were ticking by and I heard a sound at the door which I could not at first understand. It was as if a piece of furniture was bumping against the wall of the narrow staircase. Then, when I heard Marguerite starting to cry again, I realized what was happening: they were bringing up my coffin.

"You're too early," said Madame Gabin, crossly. "Put it down behind the bed."

What was the time, then? Possibly nine o'clock. So the coffin had already arrived. I could see it dimly through my blurred eyes, a brand-new coffin made of roughly planed boards. Oh God! Was this the end? Was I going to be carried out in this wooden box which they'd put down at the head of my bed?

But one final and pleasant surprise was still in store for me: despite her grief, Marguerite insisted on getting me ready herself for my last journey. With the help of the old woman, she dressed me with all the tenderness of a wife and sister and as she slipped each garment over my body, I could feel her again holding me in her arms. Overcome by emotion, she kept stopping, hugging me tightly and bathing my face in tears. How I longed to return her caresses and cry out: "I'm alive!" but I continued to lie there, an inert mass of flesh.

"I shouldn't do that, it's a waste," the old woman kept saying.

"No, I want to dress him in his best," Marguerite replied brokenly.

I realized that she was dressing me as if for our wedding. I had kept those clothes, intending to wear them only on very special occasions. Now she sank back exhausted into the armchair.

Suddenly I heard Simoneau's voice. No doubt he had just come into the room.

"They're downstairs," he said quietly.

"About time too," replied Madame Gabin, lowering her voice as well. "Tell them to come up, we mustn't linger."

"I'm afraid of the effect on his poor wife."

The old woman seemed to be thinking. Then she said:

"Look, Monsieur Simoneau, you make her go into my room. She mustn't stay here. It'll be a kindness to her... Meanwhile, we can get everything done here in a jiffy."

Her words went straight to my heart and you can imagine the agonies I went through during the ensuing struggle. Simoneau went up to Marguerite and begged her not to stay in the room.

"For pity's sake," he said imploringly, "please come with me, there's no point in exposing yourself to unnecessary suffering."

"No, I won't," my wife kept saying. "I'm going to stay here until the end. Don't forget that he's all I've got in the world and when he's gone, I shall be all alone."

While this was happening, Madame Gabin was standing beside the bed, muttering to the young man:

"Go and pick her up and take her away in your arms."

Was Simoneau going to do as she suggested and carry her off like that? All of a sudden she cried out. I made a frantic effort to get to my feet but all my strength had deserted me. So I lay there, so paralysed that I couldn't even open my eyelids to see what was taking place under my very nose. The struggle continued as my wife clung to the furniture, crying:

"Let me go, Monsieur, oh please let me go, I want to stay here!"

He must have been holding her tightly, for she started whimpering like a child. He carried her off protesting and as her sobs died away, I could see the two of them in my mind's eye; strong and powerful as he was, he was lifting her off the ground and holding her close against his chest, while she had her arms round his neck, sobbing in a heart-rending fashion but eventually giving up the struggle and letting him take her away where he wanted.

"Heavens above! That wasn't easy," murmured Madame Gabin. "Well, now we've cleared the stage, let's get on with the job."

In my jealous rage, Simoneau's action in carrying her off in this way seemed like a criminal abduction. I hadn't been able to see Marguerite since the day before, but I had been able to hear her and now I couldn't even do that. She'd been taken away from me even before I was under the ground. And he was alone with her behind the partition, consoling her, perhaps even kissing her.

The door opened again and there was the sound of heavy footsteps in the room.

"Let's be quick before she comes back," Madame Gabin was saying.

She was addressing some unknown persons whose only reply was to grunt.

"I'm not a relative, you know, just a neighbour. There's nothing in it for me… I'm seeing to all this out of sheer kindness of heart. And it's not a cheerful job, either. I spent the night in this room and it wasn't all that warm at about four o'clock in the morning, I can tell you. Well, I've always been stupid, I'm too kind to people."

At this point they pulled the coffin into the room. I realized what was happening and that I was doomed because I was not going to be able to wake up. My mind became confused; a black fog was swirling round inside my head. I was so overcome by exhaustion that it was almost a relief to realize that there was no further hope for me.

"They haven't been mean with their wood," remarked one undertaker in a hoarse voice. "It's too long."

"Ah well, he'll be more comfortable," replied another voice jokingly.

I wasn't a heavy man, which pleased them, since there were three flights of stairs to go down. Just as they were catching hold of my shoulders and feet, Madame Gabin suddenly exclaimed, crossly:

"You naughty little girl! You're always poking your nose in where you shouldn't! I'll teach you to peep round the corner!"

It was Dédé pushing her untidy mop of hair round the door to have a look at the man being put into his wooden box. There was the sound of two loud slaps, followed by a burst of tears, and when her mother came back into the room, she talked about her daughter while the men were putting me into the coffin:

"She's ten years old and she's not a bad little girl but she's far too nosey. I don't spank her a lot but she's got to learn to do as she's told."

"Oh, all little girls are like that, you know," said one of the men. "When there's a dead person in the house, they always keep hanging around."

I was lying comfortably stretched out and but for my left arm, which was pressing against one of the sides, I could have imagined myself still on the bed. As they had pointed out, I fitted in very nicely, because I was so short.

"Wait a second!" exclaimed Madame Gabin. "I promised his wife to put a pillow under his head."

But the undertakers were in a hurry and pushed the pillow under very roughly. One of them was swearing as he looked for his hammer. They had left it downstairs and had to go down to fetch it. The lid was placed on and all of a sudden my whole body was jarred as the first nail was driven in with two blows of the hammer. So this really was the end; my life was finished... And quickly the nails were driven home with sharp, repeated blows of the hammer. They worked skilfully and unconcernedly, like men nailing the lid on a box of fruit. Henceforth, every sound reaching me was muffled and long drawn out, with a strange echo, as if the deal coffin had turned into a big sounding box. The last words I heard in the bedroom in the Rue Dauphine were spoken by Madame Gabin:

"Go down gently and be careful of the second-floor banister, it's loose."

They were carrying me away. I felt as though I was being tossed in a stormy sea, but from this moment onwards, my memories are very vague. However, I do recall that my only concern, a sort of instinctive and quite absurd one, was to try to memorize the route to the cemetery. I didn't know a single Paris street or the exact location of the principal cemeteries that I had occasionally heard mentioned, but this didn't prevent me from concentrating all my remaining thoughts on working out whether we were turning left or right. The hearse was bumping me about over the paving stones. All around there was the rumble of traffic and the sound of footsteps of passers-by which created a confused murmur, magnified by the sounding-board effect of the coffin. At first, I was able to follow the route fairly clearly. Then we stopped and I was moved; I realized that we had reached the church. But as soon as the hearse set off again, I lost all sense of direction. A peal of bells informed me that we were passing close to a church, while a gentler, more continuous rumble made me think that we were going along beside an esplanade. I felt like a condemned man being led to execution, awaiting the final blow which never came.

We stopped again and I was lifted out of the hearse. And now everything happened very quickly. The sounds had all ceased and I could sense that I was in a deserted spot, under some trees and the sweep of the sky. No doubt there were some mourners, people from the hotel, Simoneau and a few others, because I could hear whispering. There was some chanting and a priest mumbled some Latin. Then, for a couple of minutes, there was nothing to be heard but the sound of footsteps. Suddenly, I felt myself sinking and ropes were vibrating against the sides of the coffin like a bow playing on a cracked double bass. This was the end. A staggering blow, like the bursting of a shell, exploded just to the left of my head; a second blow exploded at my feet; a third, even stronger, struck over my stomach. This last one was so loud that I thought it had split the coffin in two. And then I lost consciousness.

4

HOW LONG I REMAINED IN THAT STATE I find it impossible to say. For a person completely unconscious, a second is the same as eternity. I no longer existed. Then, gradually, a confused feeling of being alive revived. I was still in a sort of sleep but I had started dreaming. Against the impenetrable darkness blocking my future, a nightmare was taking shape. It was a weird figment of my imagination and one which had often tormented me in the past when, with my horrible propensity for inventing dire catastrophes, I would lie awake, open-eyed, savouring the masochistic pleasure of dreaming up disasters.

Thus I would imagine that my wife was expecting me somewhere, I think in Guérande, and that I was on my way by train. Just as the train was going through a tunnel, there was a frightful rumbling sound, like a clap of thunder: it was a double landslide. The train was completely undamaged and every compartment intact, but the roof of the tunnel had collapsed at both ends and so we found ourselves trapped in the middle of a mountain, immured by the rock fall. We were condemned to a horrible, lingering death, with no hope of help, for it would take a month to unblock the tunnel, using powerful equipment and extreme care. We were imprisoned in a sort of cellar without any exit. The death of every passenger was merely a matter of time.

As I have said, my imagination was frequently exercised by such horrible situations. I would think up all sorts of variants. I peopled my drama with a full cast of men, women and children, a hundred or so, and this crowd of people gave me scope for an endless variety of episodes. There was a certain amount of food on the train but this supply was quickly exhausted and without quite resorting to cannibalism, the starving passengers fought like tigers over the few remaining scraps of bread. An old man, at his last gasp, was brutally punched and driven away, a mother fought like a tigress to hold onto a few mouthfuls of food for her child. In my own compartment, two young newly-weds had given up hope and lay motionless and dying in each other's arms. The track itself was clear and passengers were able to climb down and prowl along the train like wild beasts in search of their prey. Class distinctions had vanished; one very rich man, a senior government official it was whispered, was crying on a workman's shoulder and addressing him like a brother. The lights had soon failed and the furnace of the locomotive had finally gone out. As we moved from carriage to carriage, we groped our way along the wheels to avoid bumping into each other until we reached the engine, which we could recognize from its cold piston rod and its bulging sides, a slumbering, impotent giant lying motionless in the darkness. You could imagine no more frightening spectacle than this train totally immured underground like someone buried alive, with all its passengers dying one by one.

I used to revel in every tiny horrible detail. The darkness was pierced by screams and suddenly a man, whom I hadn't seen and hadn't realized was sitting beside me, slumped down against my shoulder. But it was the cold and lack of air which was really affecting me now. Never had I felt so cold; a mantle of snow seemed to be settling on my shoulders, my head was reeling in the clammy air and at the same time I felt that I was being stifled as the roof of rock seemed to be collapsing and pressing down on to my chest. The whole mass of the mountain was crushing me. But a cry of relief rang out. For some time we had been imagining that we could hear dull thuds in the distance and hopes were beginning to rise that they had started to dig us out. But now relief was at hand from another quarter – one of our number had just discovered an air shaft in the tunnel and we all ran over to look at it. A blue patch could be seen at the top, no larger than a blob of sealing wax, but this tiny patch of blue filled us with joy. We stood craning our necks endeavouring to snatch a breath of fresh air. We could clearly distinguish some black dots frantically working; they must surely be workmen setting up a winch to haul us to safety. A cry burst from our throats. We were saved! We were saved! Everyone was shouting and waving their arms towards this tiny blue patch.

It was the sound of these shouts which woke me up. Where was I? Was I still in the tunnel? I was lying stretched out and I could feel my body enclosed between walls on both sides. I tried to sit up but my head struck violently against some hard object. I must be surrounded by rock on all sides. And the blue patch had disappeared; the sky was no longer visible, even in the distance. I was still suffocating and my teeth were chattering as a shiver ran through my whole body.

Suddenly everything came back to me. My hair bristled with horror and an icy tremor shook me from head to foot as the dreadful truth flooded into my brain. Had I finally been freed from the paralysis that had held me stiff and corpselike in its grip for so long? Yes, I could move and I ran my trembling hands along the sides of the coffin. There remained one final test: I opened my mouth and tried to speak, instinctively calling Marguerite's name. But my call turned into a scream and my voice echoed round the coffin in a terrifying, ear-splitting shriek. Oh dear God! Could it be true? I could move and I could call out that I was alive, but there was no one to hear me, I was entombed under the ground...

I made one final effort to control myself and gather my wits about me. Wasn't there some way of escape? I started to relive my dream; my brain was still reeling and in my imagination the air shaft and the patch of blue sky were mingling with the reality of the hole in which I was suffocating. With wild, staring eyes I probed the darkness. Perhaps I might be able to see a slit, a hole, a sliver of light? But in the gloom all around me, I could see only a stream of twinkling lights and specks of red which spread out and vanished, leaving a black, bottomless abyss. Then my brain cleared and I thrust the stupid nightmare from my mind. If I was to save myself, I should need all my wits.

First of all, my greatest danger seemed to be the ever-increasing stuffiness which was threatening to suffocate me. No doubt I had been able to do without air for so long because my physical functions had been paralysed, but now that my heart had started beating and my lungs were breathing again, if I didn't free myself as quickly as possible, I should be asphyxiated. I was also suffering from the cold and I was afraid of becoming numb and dying, like people who topple over into a snowdrift and never climb out.

While I kept on reminding myself that I must remain quite calm, I could feel waves of panic sweeping over me. So in an effort to pull myself together, I tried to recall everything I knew about methods of burial. I must have been buried in a five-year concession and that effectively put paid to one of my hopes – for I had noticed that as each hole was filled up in the paupers' graves, the end of the most recent coffin was left exposed. Had that been the case, I should only have needed to break through one plank to escape, whereas if I was in a hole that had been filled up to the top, there was a tremendous weight of earth above me and this would prove a formidable obstacle. Hadn't I read somewhere that in Paris graves were dug out to a depth of six feet? How could I get through such an enormous thickness of earth? Even should I be able to split the lid of my coffin open, wouldn't the earth come pouring in like fine sand and fill my nose and mouth so that I would die a second, horrible death, drowned in slime?

However, I carefully explored the space all around me. The coffin was a large one and I had no difficulty in moving my arms. As far as I could discover, there were no gaps in the lid and though the left and right sides of the coffin were only roughly planed, they were tough and solid. I bent my arm back across my chest and felt beyond my head. There, in the end plank, I discovered a knot that gave a little when I pressed against it. So I laboriously rocked it until at last it fell out. Then, inserting my finger, I felt the earth beyond; it was a thick, wet clay. But that got me no further. I even regretted having removed the knot, as the slime might be able to seep though the hole. I decided to try another experiment and tapped all round the coffin to see if there might perhaps be a hollow space on one side or the other. But the sound was the same wherever I tapped. However, when I gently knocked the end of the coffin, the sound seemed to me to be higher pitched, but this could have been caused by the shape or method of construction.

Then, with my arms held above my chest, I began gently pushing with my fists. The lid did not move an inch. Next I tried bracing myself on my back and feet and pushing with my knees. There was not even a creak. Finally, exerting my full strength and using every muscle in my body, I pushed until my bones cracked and then lashed out until I was bruised all over. It was then that I lost my head.

Until now I'd been determined to remain clear-headed and control the bursts of impotent rage which threatened to sweep over me like the fumes in a drunkard's head. Above all, I had been resisting the temptation to shout because I realized that if I started shouting, I should be lost. And now, all at once, I began shouting and screaming. I had reached the limits of my endurance; scream upon scream burst from my lips until I could scream no more. I was calling for help in a voice that I could not recognize as my own, becoming more hysterical with every shout I uttered. I was screaming that I didn't want to die, while at the same time I was scratching at the boards with my nails and writhing convulsively like a trapped wolf.

I don't know how long this outburst of hysteria lasted but I can still feel those hard, unyielding wooden planks which I was vainly trying to force my way through and still hear my screams and sobs reverberating inside them. A last flicker of reason was urging me to control myself but I was powerless to do so.

In the end I lapsed into a state of nervous exhaustion. Barely conscious, I lay painfully waiting to die. The coffin was as solid as a rock: I should never manage to break it open, and the certainty of this left me completely sapped of energy and of the courage to make any further attempt. And now another ordeal was added to the cold and lack of air: the pangs of hunger which soon became unbearable. Through the knothole, I tried to gather a few pinches of earth which I then swallowed: they merely increased my sufferings. I took hold of my arm in my clenched teeth and sucked at my skin, tempted to bite into my flesh and drink my blood, but I could not quite bring myself to do it.

By now, I was longing to die. Till then I had always had a horror at the thought of annihilation and now I had reached the stage of hoping for it, even praying for it. To be completely wiped out! And it would be impossible for it to be too complete. How childish I'd been to be afraid of that sleep without dreams, that black stillness that would last for ever! Death would be a happy release, because it would, in one fell swoop, obliterate all consciousness for all eternity. To be able to become like a stone, a handful of dust, simply to cease to be!

Yet my groping hands were still continuing automatically to feel around the inside of my coffin. Suddenly, something pricked my left thumb and the slight pain roused me from my torpor. What could it be? I felt again and realized that it was a nail which the undertakers had hammered in askew without noticing, and which had missed the edge of the coffin. It was a very long nail with a very sharp point. The head of the nail was in the lid but I could feel that it was loose. Now I had only one thought in my mind: I must get that nail. Holding my right hand above my waist, I began to rock the nail to and fro. It was no easy task, for the nail was not very loose. I had to change hands frequently, because my other hand was awkwardly placed and quickly became tired. While I was working desperately at the nail, a plan was taking shape in my head whereby it could prove to be my salvation. I must get it out, at all costs. But could I do it in the short time left to me? I was weak from hunger and forced to stop, because my head was reeling and my hands had lost their strength. My mind was in a whirl. I had already sucked up the drops of blood oozing from my pricked thumb, now I bit hard into my arm and drank my blood... Spurred on by the pain and invigorated by the taste of this warm, salty wine moistening my lips, I set to work again with both hands. At last I managed to free the nail and pull it inside the coffin.

It was at this moment that I realized that I was going to succeed. My plan was simple. I jabbed the point of the nail into the lid of the coffin and dragged it in a straight line as far as I could, and I kept on moving the nail backwards and forwards to score as deep a groove as possible. My hands became stiff and sore but with the force of despair I kept doggedly on. When I judged that the groove was deep enough, I turned over on to my front and bracing myself on elbows and knees, I pushed up with my back. I heard the lid creak but it refused to split. The groove was obviously not deep enough, so I turned on to my back and started scraping away with the nail once more. It was laborious work. After a while I turned over again and made another attempt, and this time the lid split from top to bottom...

Well, I was not yet safe but hope was beginning to stir. I stopped pushing and lay completely still for fear that the soil might slide down and bury me. I planned to use the lid as a sort of shield whilst I tried to hollow out a shaft in the earth. Unfortunately this proved difficult in the extreme, for the heavy lumps of clay kept slipping down and pressing on the lid, making it impossible for me to move it. I would never reach the surface, for these lumps were already weighing down so strongly on my back that my face was being thrust against the bottom of the coffin. Just as I was beginning to panic, I thought, as I stretched out, preparatory to bracing myself, that I could feel the end of the coffin giving way under my pressure. I kicked hard against it with my heels, thinking there might be a hollow space there, where they were in the process of digging a grave.

Suddenly I felt that my feet were free. My intuition had proved correct: an open grave had recently been dug out there and all that I now had to do was to break through a narrow bank of earth. I slid out into the open. Thank God! I was saved!

For a moment I lay on my back looking up at the sky. It was night time and the stars were shining in the dark, velvety, blue sky. The wind was rising, bringing warm gusts of spring air and a scent of trees. Thank God! I was saved, I could breathe, I was warm and I was weeping tears of joy. I clasped my hands together and in a broken voice offered a prayer of thanks to Heaven. How wonderful it was to be alive!

5

M Y FIRST THOUGHT was to make my way to the caretaker of the cemetery and get him to arrange for me to be taken home. But on second thoughts, still confused in my mind, I hesitated. Wouldn't everybody be frightened when they saw me? And why be in such a hurry, now that everything was going to be all right? Apart from the small wound in my left arm where I had bitten myself, there was nothing wrong with me and indeed the slight fever brought on by this wound was stimulating me and giving me an unexpected feeling of energy. I would certainly be able to walk without help.

So I decided to take my time, for my mind was still in something of a muddle. In the grave next to mine, I had noticed the gravediggers' spades and the thought came to me that I ought to make good the damage I had done and fill up the hole in such a way that nobody would notice my resurrection. At the time I had no clear idea in mind, I merely felt that it was pointless to publicize what had happened; in fact, I felt rather ashamed of being still alive when everyone thought I was dead. It took me less than half an hour to cover up all traces of my escape.

I jumped out of the grave. What a wonderful night it was! The cemetery was plunged in silence and the dark trees were casting still shadows on the white gravestones. As I was trying to find my sense of direction,* I saw that one half of the sky was glowing as if on fire. That must be Paris and I set off in that direction, keeping in the shadow of the overhanging branches of an avenue of trees. But I had barely gone fifty yards before I was forced to stop and sit down, out of breath, on a stone bench. Only then did I examine myself closely: I was completely dressed, even down to my shoes; the only thing missing was a hat. How I blessed Marguerite's sense of piety in having me properly clothed! And the sudden memory of Marguerite brought me to my feet: I wanted to see her.

At the end of the avenue, my way was blocked by a wall. I clambered up on to a gravestone and, hanging from the coping, I let myself drop on the far side. I fell heavily. Picking myself up, I followed for a few minutes a wide, deserted street that ran beside the cemetery. I had not the slightest idea where I was but I kept saying to myself determinedly that I would find my way back into Paris and then certainly be able to get to the Rue Dauphine. Some people went by but, seized by a sudden feeling of distrust, I didn't speak to them; I didn't feel that I wanted to confide in anyone at the moment. I realize now that I was already suffering from a high fever and becoming delirious. In the end, just as I was coming out into a main street, I was overcome by dizziness and fell heavily on the pavement.

Here there is a gap in my life. I remained unconscious for three weeks. When I finally came to, I was lying in a strange bedroom. I was being looked after by a man who merely told me that he had picked me up one morning in the Boulevard Montparnasse and taken me back to his house. He was a retired doctor. When I thanked him, he replied briefly that my case had intrigued him and he had wanted to observe me. Moreover, during the first few weeks of my convalescence, he would not allow me to ask any questions. Nor, later on, did he ask me any. I stayed in bed for another week; my mind was still unclear and I did not even try to go back over all that had happened, for I found it both tiring and saddening. I felt afraid and in no mood to talk. I'd go and see how things were once I was fit enough to leave the house. Perhaps, during my delirium, I might have blurted out a name but the doctor never referred to anything that I might have said. He was as discreet as he was kind.

Meanwhile, summer had come and one morning in June I received permission, at last, to go for a short walk. It was a superb day, with a cheerful sun making the old streets of Paris look young again. I went slowly along, asking the way to the Rue Dauphine from passers-by at every street crossing. At last, I reached my goal but I had difficulty in recognizing the furnished hotel in which we had stayed. I was like a scared child. If I showed myself to Marguerite too unexpectedly, I was afraid she would be overcome by shock. Perhaps the best thing would be to warn old Madame Gabin first of all? But I didn't like the idea of anyone coming between Marguerite and me... I couldn't make up my mind; deep down inside me, I felt a great emptiness as if, long ago, I had sacrificed myself.

The house looked golden in the sunshine. I had recognized it by its cheap restaurant on the ground floor from which you could have meals sent up to your room. I looked up to the third floor, at the end window on the left. It was wide open. Suddenly a young woman, with her hair undone and her shift slipping off her shoulder, came to the window and rested her elbows on the sill to look out; she was immediately followed by a young man who bent over and kissed the back of her neck. It was not Marguerite. I felt no surprise; it seemed to me as if it were all part of a dream, like so many other things that I was about to experience.

For a second, I stood hesitating in the street, thinking I might go up and question this happy young couple of lovers who were still laughing and enjoying the sun. Eventually, I decided to go into the little ground-floor restaurant. I felt sure that, with my hollow cheeks and the beard which had grown during my illness, no one would recognize me. Just as I was taking my seat at a table, who should appear but Madame Gabin herself, holding a small cup to fetch herself some coffee. She planted herself in front of the counter and started exchanging the morning's gossip with the owner's wife. I pricked up my ears.

"Well, has that poor little woman on the third floor made up her mind at last?" the woman enquired.

"What could she do?" replied Madame Gabin. "It was the best thing for her. Monsieur Simoneau has been such a good friend... He'd just completed his business, he was coming into a lot of money and he was offering to take her back with him to his home town, where she'd be able to live with one of his aunts who needs a companion."

The woman behind the bar gave a little laugh. I was hiding my face behind a newspaper; I had gone very pale and my hands were trembling.

"I imagine that it'll end in their getting married," Madame Gabin went on. "But I can assure you I haven't seen any hanky-panky... The poor dear was heartbroken over her husband and he behaved like a proper gentleman. Anyway, they left yesterday. Once she's out of mourning, they'll please themselves what they do, won't they?"

At that moment, the door leading from the hall into the restaurant swung open and Dédé came in.

"Aren't you going to come, Mummy? I've been waiting for you. Do hurry up!"

"I'm coming in a minute. Don't bother me!" her mother replied.

The girl stayed listening to the two women, like the precocious little Paris brat she was.

"And after all, the husband wasn't a patch on Monsieur Simoneau," said Madame Gabin, following her train of thought. "I didn't think much of that little whippersnapper. Always complaining... And as poor as a church mouse. No, really, a husband like that can't be much fun for a woman with some blood in her veins... And Monsieur Simoneau is rich and as strong as an ox."

"Oh yes," Dédé broke in, "I saw him having a wash one day. You should have seen his hairy arms!"

"Now just you run along!" the old woman shouted, giving her a push. "You're always sticking your nose in where it's not wanted."

Then she concluded:

"So I reckon that the husband did the right thing in dying. It's a wonderful stroke of luck."

When I found myself in the street once again, my legs could barely support me. I walked slowly away, and yet I wasn't too unhappy. I even smiled when I looked at my shadow cast by the sun: I really was weedy. It had been a queer notion of mine to marry Marguerite... And I remembered how much she'd disliked Guérande, how impatient she'd become and tired of her boring life. She had shown herself a good wife, but I had never been a proper lover for her. It was a brother she was mourning, not a husband. Why should I disturb her life again? A dead man can't be jealous... When I raised my eyes, I saw that I was standing in front of the Luxembourg gardens. I went in and sat down in the sun. I slipped into a gentle daydream. I felt full of tenderness towards Marguerite now. I could see her living in the provinces like a lady, in her little country town, very happy and loved by everyone. People would make a fuss of her. She would grow into a beauty and have three sons and two daughters... No, I'd done the right thing in dying and I'd certainly not be stupid or cruel enough to come back to life.

Since that time, I've travelled a great deal and lived in many different places. I'm a very ordinary man who's worked and fed like everyone else. I'm no longer afraid of dying, but Death doesn't seem to want anything to do with me, now that I can see no point in living. I'm afraid he's forgotten me.

Shellfish for Monsieur Chabre[*]

1

MONSIEUR CHABRE HAD ONE GREAT SORROW: he was childless. He had married a Mademoiselle Estelle Catinot (of the firm of Desvignes and Catinot). She was tall, beautiful and blonde, only eighteen years of age, but for the last four years he had been anxiously waiting, with growing dismay and wounded pride at the failure of his efforts.

Monsieur Chabre was a retired corn merchant and a very wealthy man. Despite having lived continently, as befitted a solid middle-class businessman bent on becoming a millionaire, he walked with the heavy tread of an old man, although he was only forty-five. His face, prematurely lined with financial cares, was as dull as ditchwater. And he was in despair, for a man who enjoys an investment income of fifty thousand francs a year has the right to feel surprised when he discovers that it is more difficult to become a father than to become rich.

Madame Chabre was twenty-two years old and beautiful. With her peach-like complexion and golden blonde hair curling in ringlets over her neck, she was quite adorable. Her blue-green eyes were like slumbering pools hiding depths difficult to plumb. When her husband complained of their childlessness, she would arch her supple body, emphasizing the curves of her hips and bosom, and her wry half-smile plainly said: "Is it any fault of mine?" It must be added that in her circle of friends and acquaintances, Madame Chabre was acknowledged as a young woman of perfect breeding, adequately pious and incapable of giving rise to the slightest breath of scandal, brought up, indeed, in the soundest of middle-class principles by a strict mother. Only the nostrils of her little white nose would give an occasional nervous twitch which might have given some cause for concern to anyone but a retired corn merchant.

Meanwhile the family doctor, Dr Guiraud, a large, shrewd, smiling man, had already been called in for a number of private consultations with Monsieur Chabre. He had explained to him how backward science was: you can't plant a child as you'd plant an oak, dear me no! However, not wishing to leave anyone entirely without hope, he had promised to give thought to the case. So, one July morning he called on Monsieur Chabre and said:

"You ought to go on a holiday to the sea and do some bathing. It's an excellent thing. And above all, eat shellfish, lots of shellfish. Nothing but shellfish."

Monsieur Chabre's hopes rose.

"Shellfish, doctor?" he asked eagerly. "Do you think that shell-fish?..."

"Yes, I do indeed! There's strong evidence of the success of that treatment. So you must understand, every day you eat oysters, mussels, clams, sea urchins, not forgetting crayfish and lobsters!"

Then, just as he was standing in the doorway ready to leave, he added casually:

"Don't bury yourself in some out-of-the-way place. Madame Chabre is young and needs entertainment... Go to Trouville, it's full of ozone."

Three days later, the couple were on their way. However, the ex-corn merchant had thought it pointless to go to Trouville, where he'd have to spend money hand over fist. You can eat shellfish anywhere, indeed, in an out-of-the-way resort the shellfish would be more plentiful and far cheaper. As for entertainment, there's always too much of that. After all, they weren't travelling for pleasure.

A friend had recommended the tiny resort of Pouliguen, close to Saint Nazaire, a new town with its modern, dead-straight streets still full of building sites. They visited the harbour and loitered round the streets where the shops hesitated between being tiny, gloomy village stores and large luxury grocers. At Pouliguen there was not one single house left unlet. The little timber and plaster houses, looking like garish fairground shacks, which stretched round the bay, had all been invaded by the English and rich Nantes tradesmen. Estelle pulled a wry face when she saw the queer structures in which middle-class architects had given free rein to their imagination.

The travellers were advised to spend the night in Guérande. It was a Sunday. When they arrived just before noon, even Monsieur Chabre, although not naturally a poetic person, was at first struck with ad-miration by this little jewel of a medieval town, so well preserved with its ramparts and deep gateways with battlements. Estelle looked at the drowsy little town, surrounded by its esplanades shaded by tall trees, and its charm brought a gleam into the dreamy pools of her eyes. Their carriage drove in through one of the gateways and clattered at a trot over the cobblestones of the narrow streets. The Chabres had not exchanged a word.

"What a dump!" the ex-corn merchant muttered finally. "The villages round Paris are far better built."

Their carriage halted in front of the Hôtel du Commerce, in the centre of the town, next to the church, and as they were getting out, mass was just ending. While her husband was seeing to their luggage, Estelle was intrigued to see the congregation coming out of church, many of whom were dressed in quaint costumes. Some of the men were wearing white smocks and baggy breeches; these were those who lived and worked in the vast, desolate salt marshes which stretch between Guérande and Le Croisic. Then there were the sharecroppers, a completely different species, who wore short woollen jackets and round broad-brimmed hats. But Estelle was particularly excited by the ornate costume worn by one girl. Her headdress fitted tightly round the temples and rose up to a point. Over her red bodice with wide-cuffed sleeves, she had a silk front brocaded with brightly coloured flowers. Her triple, tight-pleated, blue woollen skirt was held by a belt embroidered in gold and silver, while a long orange-coloured apron hung down, revealing her red woollen stockings and dainty yellow slippers.

"How can they allow that sort of thing!" exclaimed Monsieur Chabre. "You only see that kind of circus get-up in Brittany."

Estelle made no reply. A tall young man, about twenty years of age, was coming out of church, giving his arm to an old lady... He had a very pale complexion and honey-coloured hair; he looked very self-possessed and was something of a giant, with broad shoulders and muscular arms, despite his youth. Yet he had a delicate, gentle expression which, combined with his pink complexion and smooth skin, gave him a girlish appearance. As Estelle was staring at him, struck by his good looks, he turned his head and his eyes rested on her for a second. Then he blushed to the roots of his hair.

"Well there's someone at least who looks human. He'll make a fine cavalry officer," said Monsieur Chabre.

"That's Monsieur Hector Plougastel with his mother," said the hotel maid, hearing this remark. "He's such a kind, well-behaved boy."

While the Chabres were taking lunch, a lively argument arose at their table d'hôte. The registrar of mortgages, who took his meals at the Hôtel du Commerce, was speaking approvingly of Guérande's patriarchal way of life and particularly of the high moral standards of the young people. He claimed that it was their religious upbringing which was responsible for their good behaviour. However, a commercial traveller, who had arrived that morning with a stock of false jewellery, recounted with a grin how he'd seen young men and girls kissing behind the hedgerows as he was driving along the road. He would have liked to see what the lads of the town would have done if given the chance to meet a few attractive friendly ladies. And he went on to poke fun at religion, priests and nuns until the outraged registrar of mortgages flung down his napkin and stamped out of the room. The Chabres had gone on eating without saying a word, with the husband furious at the sort of conversation you have to listen to at a table d'hôte, while his wife sat with a placid smile on her face as if she didn't understand a word of what they were talking about.

The Chabres spent the afternoon visiting Guérande. The church of St Aubin was deliciously cool and as they walked slowly around inside, they looked up at the arched vaulting supported on slender columns which shot upwards like stone rockets, stopping to admire the strange carved capitals depicting torturers sawing their victims in two and roasting them on grills, using large bellows to fan the flames. Then they strolled round the five or six main streets of Guérande and Monsieur Chabre was confirmed in his view: it was nothing but a dump, with no trade to speak of, just one more of those antiquated medieval towns so many of which had already been knocked down. The streets were deserted, with their rows of gabled houses piled up side by side like so many tired old women. The pointed roofs, the slate-covered pepper pots and corner turrets and the weather-worn sculptures made some of the quiet backstreets of the town seem like museums drowsing in the sun. At the sight of all the lead-lit windows, a dreamy look came into Estelle's eyes; since her marriage she had taken to reading novels and she was thinking of Walter Scott.

But when the Chabres went outside the town and walked all round it, they found themselves nodding their heads appreciatively. They had to admit that it really was charming. The granite walls which completely encircled the town had weathered to a rich honey colour and were as intact as when they had been built, though ivy and honeysuckle now draped the battlements. Shrubs had grown on the towers flanking the ramparts and their brightly coloured flowers, golden gorse and flaming gillyflower, glowed under the clear blue sky. Grassy walks under shady age-old oaks extended all around the town. They picked their way carefully, as though stepping on a carpet, as they walked along beside the former moat, partly filled in and further on turning into weed-covered stagnant pools in whose mysteriously glinting surface were mirrored the white trunks of birch trees growing close up to the walls amongst the wispy green undergrowth. Rays of light shone through the trees lighting up hidden nooks and crannies, the deep-set posterns where the peace of centuries was disturbed only by the sudden leaps of frightened frogs.

"There are ten towers, I've just been counting them," exclaimed Monsieur Chabre when they had come round to their starting point.

He had been particularly struck by the four gateways with their long narrow entrances through which only one carriage could pass at a time. Wasn't it quite absurd to keep yourself shut in like that in the nineteenth century? If he'd been in charge he'd have knocked down the fortress-like gateways, with their useless loopholes and such thick walls that you could have built a couple of six-storey dwellings on their sites.

"Not to mention all the building materials you'd get from demolishing the ramparts," he added.

They were standing in the Mall, a spacious raised esplanade which curved in a quarter-circle from the eastern to the southern gateways. Estelle was gazing pensively over the striking panorama which spread out for miles beyond the roofs of the suburbs. First of all there came a dense, dark green belt of gnarled shrubs and pine trees leaning sideways from the force of the winds coming in from the ocean. Then followed the immense plain of desolate salt marshes, flat and bare, with their square patches of seawater gleaming like mirrors beside the little heaps of salt which shone white against the grey expanse of sand. Further on, at the skyline, she could make out the deep blue of the Atlantic on which three tiny sails looked like white swallows.

"There's the young man we saw this morning," said Monsieur Chabre suddenly. "Doesn't he remind you of Lavière's son? If he had a humpback, he'd look exactly like him."

Estelle turned slowly round but Hector, standing at the edge of the Mall and equally absorbed in watching the sea on the distant horizon, did not seem to notice that he was being observed. The young woman started walking slowly on again. She was using her long sunshade as a walking stick but she had barely taken a dozen steps before its bow came loose. The Chabres heard a voice behind them.

"Excuse me, madam..."

Hector had retrieved the bow.

"Thank you very much indeed," said Estelle with her quiet smile.

He really was a nice, well-mannered young man. Monsieur Chabre took to him at once and explained to him the problem facing them of finding a suitable resort, and even asked for Hector's advice.

Hector was very shy.

"I don't think you'll find the sort of place you're looking for either at Le Croisic or Le Batz," he said, pointing to the church spires of these two little towns on the horizon. "I think your best plan would be to go to Piriac."

He gave them some details: Piriac was about seven miles away, he had an uncle living on the outskirts. Finally, in reply to questions by Monsieur Chabre, he said that there were plenty of shellfish to be found there.

The young woman was poking the point of her sunshade into the short turf. The young man kept his eyes averted as though embarrassed to look her in the face.

"Guérande is an extremely pretty place," she said finally in her soft voice.

"Oh yes, extremely," stammered Hector, suddenly devouring her with his eyes.

2

ONE MORNING, three days after settling in at Piriac, Monsieur Chabre was standing on the platform at the end of the sea wall protecting the tiny harbour, stolidly keeping watch over Estelle who was bathing. At the moment she was floating on her back. The sun was already very hot and, decorously dressed in black frock coat and felt hat, he was warding off its rays by means of a sunshade with a green lining. He looked every inch the holiday visitor.

"Is the water warm?" he enquired, feigning interest in his wife's bathing.

"Lovely!" she replied, turning on to her front.

Monsieur Chabre was terrified of the water and never ventured into it. He would explain that his doctors had explicitly forbidden him to bathe in the sea. When a wave so much as came towards his shoes on the beach, he would start back in alarm as if he were being faced by some vicious animal baring its teeth. In any case, seawater would have disturbed his decorum; he looked on it as dirty and disgusting.

"So it really is warm?" he enquired again, his head swimming from the heat. He felt both drowsy and uncomfortable standing at the end of the sea wall.

Estelle did not bother to reply: she was busy swimming a dog-paddle. In the water, she was as fearless as a boy and would swim for hours, to the dismay of her husband who felt it incumbent on him to wait at the water's edge. At Piriac Estelle had found the sort of bathing she liked; she despised gently shelving beaches where you have to walk a long way out before the water comes up to your waist. She would go to the end of the sea wall wrapped in her flannel bathrobe, slip it off and take a header without a second thought. She used to say that she needed fifteen feet of water to avoid striking her head on the rocky bottom. Her skirtless one-piece bathing costume clung to her tall figure and the long blue belt tied round her waist emphasized the graceful curve of her firm, full hips. Moving through the clear water, with her hair caught up in a rubber bathing cap from which a few strands of blonde curls were escaping, she looked like some sleek agile dolphin with a disconcertingly pink woman's face.

Monsieur Chabre had been standing in the sweltering hot sun for a good quarter of an hour. He had already consulted his watch three times. Finally he risked a timid comment:

"You've been in a long time, my dear. Oughtn't you to come out? You'll get tired, bathing so long."

"But I've only just gone in," the young woman replied. "I'm as warm as toast."

Then, turning on her back again, she added:

"If you're bored, you needn't stay. I don't need you."

He objected with a shake of his head, pointing out how quickly a danger could arise; Estelle smiled at the thought; her husband would be a fat lot of good if she were suddenly attacked by cramp. But at this moment her attention was drawn to the other side of the sea wall, towards the bay that lay to the left of the village.

"Good gracious!" she exclaimed. "What's happening over there? I'm going to have a look."

And she swam off with a long, powerful breaststroke.

"Estelle, come back!" shouted Monsieur Chabre. "You know I can't bear it when you take risks!"

But Estelle was not listening and he had to possess himself in patience. Standing on tiptoe to watch the white speck of his wife's straw hat, he merely transferred his sunshade to the other hand; he was finding the stifling heat more and more unbearable.

"What on earth has she seen?" he muttered to himself. "Oh, it's that thing floating over there... A bit of rubbish, I expect. A bunch of seaweed, perhaps? Or a barrel. No, it can't be, it's moving."

Then he suddenly recognized what it was:

"It's a man swimming!"

However, after a few strokes, Estelle had also recognized perfectly well that it was a man. She therefore stopped swimming straight towards him, since that seemed hardly the proper thing. But she mischievously decided not to swim back to the sea wall and continued to make for the open sea, pleased to be able to show how bold she was. She pursued her course, pretending not to notice the other swimmer, who was now gradually coming up towards her, as if being carried by the current. Thus, when she turned round to swim back to the sea wall, their paths crossed, apparently quite fortuitously.

"I hope you are well, madam?" the young man enquired politely.

"Oh, it's you!" Estelle exclaimed brightly.

And she added with a smile:

"What a small world it is, isn't it?"

It was young Hector de Plougastel. He was still very shy, very well built and looked very pink in the water. For a moment they swam without speaking, maintaining a decent distance between each other. In order to converse, they had to raise their voices. However, Estelle felt that she ought to be polite.

"We're very grateful to you for having told us about Piriac... My husband is delighted with it."

"Isn't that your husband standing by himself on the sea wall?" asked Hector.

"Yes," she replied.

Silence fell again. They were watching her husband who looked like a tiny black insect above the sea. Very intrigued, Monsieur Chabre was craning his neck even more and wondering who the man was whose acquaintance his wife had just made in the middle of the sea. There was no doubt about it, his wife was definitely chatting with him. It must be one of their Paris friends. But running his mind over the list of their friends, he could not think of one bold enough to swim so far out. And so he waited, aimlessly twirling his sunshade round in his hand.

"Yes," Hector was explaining to the attractive Madame Chabre, "I've come over to spend a few days in my uncle's chateau which you can see over there, halfway up the hill. So for my daily swim, I set off from that piece of land jutting out opposite the terrace and swim to the sea wall and back. Just over a mile in all. It's wonderful exercise... But you're a very daring swimmer, I don't think I've ever met such a daring lady swimmer."

"Oh I've been splashing about in the water ever since I was a little girl," said Estelle. "Water doesn't have any secrets for me, we're old friends."

To avoid having to talk so loudly, they were gradually drawing closer to each other. On this beautiful warm morning, the sea was like one vast piece of watered silk, drowsing in the sun. Parts were as smooth as satin, separated by narrow bands of shimmering water, stretching out into the distance, currents looking like creases in a cloth. Once they were closer to each other, their conversation took a more intimate turn.

"What a superb day!" And Hector began to point out several landmarks along the coast. That village over there, less than a mile away, was Port aux Loups; opposite was the Morbihan, with its white cliffs standing out sharply as in some watercolour; and finally, in the other direction, towards the open sea, the island of Dumet could be seen as a grey speck set in the blue sea. Each time Hector pointed, Estelle stopped swimming for a second, charmed to see these distant sights from sea level against the infinite backdrop of the limpid sky. When she looked towards the sun, her eyes were dazzled and the sea seemed as though transformed into a boundless Sahara, with the blinding sunlight bleaching the immense stretch of sandy beach.

"Isn't it lovely," she murmured. "Isn't it really gorgeous!"

She turned over and relaxed, lying back motionless in the water with her arms stretched out sideways. Her gleaming white thighs and arms floated on the surface.

"So you were born in Guérande?" she asked.

"Yes," he replied. "I've only been once as far as Nantes."

In order to talk more comfortably, Hector now also turned over on to his back. He gave details of his upbringing, for which his mother had been responsible: a narrowly devout woman whose values had been the traditional ones of the old aristocracy. He had had a priest as tutor who had taught him more or less what he would have learnt in a private school, plus large amounts of catechism and heraldry. He rode, fenced and took a great deal of exercise. And with all this, he seemed as innocent as a babe in arms. He went to mass every week, never read novels and when he reached his majority, would be marrying a very plain cousin.

"Goodness me! So you're only just twenty," exclaimed Estelle, casting an astonished glance at this young colossus. Her maternal instincts were aroused; this fine specimen of the Breton race intrigued her. But as they continued floating on their backs, lost in contemplation of the transparent blue sky and quite oblivious of land, they drifted so close together that he slightly knocked against her.

"Oh, I'm sorry," he said.

And dived and came to the surface five yards away. She burst into laughter and began to swim again.

"You boarded me!" she cried.

He was very red in the face. He swam nearer again, watching her slyly. Under her broad-brimmed straw hat, she seemed to him delightful. He could see nothing but her face and her dimpled chin dipping into the water. A few drops of water dripped from the blonde curls escaping from beneath her bathing cap, and glistened like pearls on the down of her cheeks. He could imagine nothing more charming than the smile and pretty face of this young woman swimming ahead of him, gently splashing and leaving behind her merely a silvery trail.

When he noticed that Estelle realized that she was being watched and was amused at the odd figure he was certainly cutting, Hector blushed an even deeper red. He tried to find something to say:

"Your husband seems to be getting impatient."

"Oh, I don't think so," she replied calmly. "He's used to being kept waiting when I'm having a swim."

In fact, Monsieur Chabre was becoming restless. He kept taking four steps forwards, turning round and taking four steps backward, twirling his sunshade even more vigorously in an endeavour to cool himself.

It suddenly occurred to Estelle that perhaps her husband hadn't recognized Hector.

"I'll call out and tell him it's you," she said.

And as soon as she was in earshot of the sea wall, she shouted:

"It's the gentleman we met in Guérande who was so helpful."

"Oh good!" Monsieur Chabre shouted back. He raised his hat and said politely:

"Is the water warm?"

"Very pleasant, thank you," Hector replied.

Their bathe continued under the eye of the husband who could now hardly complain, even though his feet were excruciatingly hot from having to stand on the scorching stones. At the end of the sea wall, the water was wonderfully transparent and you could see the fine sandy bottom some two or three fathoms down, speckled here and there with pale or dark pebbles amidst waving tendrils of seaweed rising perpendicularly towards the surface. Estelle was fascinated by the clearness of the water as she swam gently along in order not to ruffle the surface, bending her head forwards until the water came up to her nose and watching the sand and the pebbles stretched out in the mysterious depths below. She was especially fascinated by the clumps of green seaweed that seemed almost like living creatures with their swaying jagged leaves resembling hundreds of crabs' claws, some of them short and sturdy growing between the rocks and others long and flexible like snakes. She kept uttering little cries each time she discovered something new:

"Oh what a big stone! It looks as if it's moving... Oh, there's a tree, a real tree with branches! Oh, there's a fish! It's darting away!"

Then suddenly she exclaimed:

"What on earth is that? It's a wedding bouquet! Do you think there really are wedding bouquets in the sea? Look, wouldn't you say that they're like orange blossoms? Oh, it's so pretty!"

Hector immediately dived and came up with a fistful of whitish seaweed which drooped and faded as soon as it left the water.

"Oh, thank you so much," said Estelle. "You shouldn't have bothered... Here you are, keep that for me, will you?" she added, throwing the bunch of seaweed at her husband's feet. For a few moments the young couple continued their swim. The air was filled with spray from their flailing arms and then, suddenly, they relaxed and glided through the water, in a circle of ripples which spread out and died away, and the surging water around them filled them with a private sensual pleasure all their own. Hector was trying to glide along in the wake of Estelle's body as it slid through the water and he could feel the warmth left by the movement of her limbs. All around, the sea had become even calmer and its pale blue had taken on a touch of pink.

"You'll be getting cold, my dear," urged Monsieur Chabre, who was dripping with sweat himself.

"All right, I'm coming out," she replied.

And so she did, pulling herself up quickly with the help of a chain hanging down the sloping side of the sea wall. Hector must have been watching for her to climb out, but when he raised his head on hearing the spatter of drops she left behind, she was already on the platform and wrapped in her bathing robe. He looked so surprised and disconcerted that she had to smile as she gave a little shiver, and she gave a little shiver because she knew that she was charming when she did so, draped in her bathrobe with her tall figure standing out against the sky.

The young man reluctantly took his leave.

"We hope to see you again," the husband said.

And while Estelle ran back along the sea wall, watching Hector's head disappearing over the water as he swam back across the bay, Monsieur Chabre walked after her with the bunch of seaweed gathered by the young man solemnly held out in order to avoid wetting his frock coat.

3

IN PIRIAC the Chabres had rented the first floor of a large house overlooking the sea. As the village had no decent restaurants, they had had to take on a local woman to cook for them. And a queer sort of cook she was, producing roasts burnt to a cinder and such peculiar-looking sauces that Estelle preferred to stick to bread. But as Monsieur kept pointing out, they hadn't come to enjoy the pleasures of the table. In any case, he hardly touched either the roasts or the sauces for he was stuffing himself, morning, noon and night, on shellfish of every description, with the determination of someone taking medicine. The unfortunate thing was that he loathed these strange, oddly shaped creatures, having been brought up on a typical middle-class diet of insipid hygienic food, and retained his childish predilection for sweet things. The queer flavour and salty fieriness of shellfish burnt his tongue and made him pull a face every time he swallowed them, but in his eagerness to become a father, he would have swallowed the shells themselves.

"Estelle, you're not eating any," he would exclaim, for he insisted that she should eat as many as he and when Estelle pointed out that Dr Guiraud hadn't mentioned her, Monsieur Chabre replied that, logically, they should both submit to the same treatment. Estelle pursed her lips, let her bright eyes rest for a moment on her husband's pasty paunch and could not repress a slight smile which deepened the dimples on her cheek. She made no comment, for she did not like hurting people's feelings. Having discovered that there was a local oyster bed, she even consented to eat a dozen of them at every meal, not because she, personally, needed oysters, but she adored them.

Life in Piriac was monotonous and soporific. There were only three families of holidaymakers: a wholesale grocer from Nantes, a former lawyer from Guérande, as naive as he was deaf, and a couple from Angers who spent all day waist-deep in the sea, fishing. The restricted company would hardly be described as boisterous. They would greet each other each time they met but made no attempt to further their acquaintance. The greatest excitement was provided by the occasional dogfight on the deserted quayside.

Accustomed to the noise and bustle of Paris, Estelle would have been bored to death had Hector not taken to calling every day. After going for a walk with Monsieur Chabre along the coast, he had become a firm friend of the older man who in an expansive moment had confided to him the purpose of his trip, in the discreetest possible terms, in order not to shock the modest young man's delicate sensibilities. When he mentioned the scientific reason for eating such vast quantities of shellfish, Hector was so amazed that he forgot to blush and looked him up and down without even bothering to conceal his surprise that a man might need to submit to such a diet. Nevertheless, the following morning he presented him with a small basketful of clams which the ex-corn merchant accepted with obvious gratitude. Since then, being a highly competent all-round fisherman and familiar with every rock in the bay, Hector had never come to the house without bringing some shellfish: superb mussels which he had gathered at low tide; sea urchins which he cut open and cleaned, pricking his fingers in the process; and limpets which he prised off the rocks with the tip of his knife; in a word, every kind of shellfish, often bearing barbarous names, and which he would never have dreamt of eating himself. No longer having to spend a penny on his diet, Monsieur Chabre was profuse in his thanks.

Hector now had a permanent pretext to come to the Chabres' flat. Every time he arrived carrying his little basket, he would make the same remark when he saw Estelle:

"I'm bringing your husband some shellfish."

And the couple would exchange a smile with a glint in their half-closed eyes; they found Monsieur Chabre's shellfish rather funny.

Estelle now discovered that Piriac was full of charm. Every day after her bathe, she would go for a walk with Hector; her husband lumbered along, heavy-footed, some distance behind; they often went too fast for him. Hector would point out examples of Piriac's more elegant past, remains of sculpture and delicately worked ornamental doors and windows. By now, what used to be a town had become merely a remote village with its narrow streets blocked by dung heaps and lined with gloomy hovels. But Estelle found the stillness and isolation so charming that she was quite prepared to step over the foul-smelling pools of liquid seeping from the middens, intrigued by every quaint old-world corner and peering inquisitively at the miserable gimcrackery lying about the mud floors of the local inhabitants' poverty-stricken houses. Hector would stop and show her the superb fig trees in the gardens, with their broad, furry, leathery leaves overhanging the low fences. They went into the narrowest little streets and leaned over the brinks of the wells to look at their smiling faces mirrored in the clear shining water below, while behind them Monsieur Chabre was busy digesting his shellfish in the shade of the green-lined sunshade which never left his grasp.

One of Estelle's great joys was to see the groups of pigs and geese roaming freely round the village. At first she had been terribly frightened of the pigs because the unpredictable movements of their fat sturdy bodies supported on such puny little feet made her continually apprehensive of being knocked into and tipped over, and they were filthy, too; with their bellies covered in black mud, they kept grunting all the time as they grubbed in the ground with their dirty snouts. But Hector assured her that pigs were the nicest sort of animals and now she was amused to see how they dashed wildly up to be fed and she loved their fresh pink skin looking like a silky evening gown, after the rain had washed them clean. The geese fascinated her, too. Two gaggles of them would often meet at the end of a lane beside a holeful of dung, coming from opposite directions. They seemed to greet each other with a click of their beaks and then joined forces to pick over the vegetable peelings floating on the surface. One of them would climb majestically on to the top of the pile, stretching out his neck and opening his eyes wide; he seemed almost to be strutting as he fluffed out the down on his breast; with his prominent yellow nose, he looked like a real king of the castle. Meanwhile the others bent their necks to peck at the ground, quacking in unison as they did so. Then, suddenly, the big goose would come squawking down from the top and the geese belonging to his group would follow him away, all poking out their necks in the same direction and waddling in time, as if they all had a limp. If a dog appeared, they would stretch their necks out even more and start hissing. At this, Estelle would clap her hands and follow the solemn procession of the two companies of geese as they made their way home like highly respectable people intent on important business. Another of her entertainments was to see both pigs and geese going down to the beach in the afternoon, just like human beings.

On her first Sunday in Piriac, Estelle felt that she ought to go to mass, something which she never did in Paris. But in the country, mass was a way of passing the time, and a chance to dress up and see people. Indeed, she met Hector there, reading out of an enormous prayer book whose binding was coming unstuck. He did not take his eyes off her, peeping over the top of his book while still reading religiously, but the glint in his eye hinted that he was smiling inwardly. As they were leaving the church, he offered his arm to Estelle as they were passing through the churchyard. In the afternoon, after Vespers, there was another spectacle, a procession to a Calvary at the other end of the village. A peasant led the way carrying a purple silk banner embroidered in gold and attached to a red shaft. Then followed two straggling lines of women. The priests were in the middle; the parish priest with his curate and the local squire's tutor were all singing at the tops of their voices. Bringing up the rear, behind a white banner carried by a brawny girl with tanned arms, there came the congregation, tramping along in their heavy clogs like a disorderly flock of sheep. As the procession passed beside the harbour, the banner and the white headdresses of the women stood out against the bright blue sea and in the sunlight, the slow procession suddenly took on a simple grandeur.

The little churchyard made Estelle feel all sentimental, although normally she didn't like sad things. On the day she had arrived, she had shuddered at the sight of all those graves underneath her window. The church was not far from the sea and the arms of the crosses all around it stretched out towards the immense sky and sea; on windy nights, the moisture-laden sea breeze seemed to be weeping on this forest of dark wooden posts. But she quickly became accustomed to this mournful sight, for the tiny churchyard had something gentle and even cheerful about it. The dead seemed to be smiling in the midst of the living, who were almost rubbing elbows with them. As the cemetery was enclosed by a low wall and thus blocked the way through the centre of Piriac, people did not think twice about stepping over the wall and following the paths which were almost invisible in the tall grass. Children used to play there, scampering about all over the granite flagstones. Cats would suddenly leap out from under the bushes and chase each other; you could often hear their amorous caterwauling and see their dark shapes with fur bristling and long tails waving in the air. It was a delightful corner covered with weeds and enormous fennel plants with broad yellow flowers; on a warm day, their heady perfume would come wafting up from the graves, filling the whole of Piriac with a scent of aniseed. And at night, how still and gentle the green graveyard was! The peace of Piriac itself seemed to be emanating from the cemetery. The darkness hid the crosses and people taking a late evening stroll would sit down on the granite benches against the wall and watch the waves rolling in almost at their feet, enjoying the salty tang of the sea carried in on the evening breeze.

One evening as Estelle was going home on Hector's arm she felt a sudden desire to go through the deserted graveyard. Monsieur Chabre thought it was a romantic whim and showed his protest by himself going along the quayside. The path was so narrow that Estelle was obliged to let go of Hector's arm. In the tall grass her skirt made a long swishing sound. The scent of fennel was so overpowering that the lovelorn cats did not run away but remained lying languidly in the undergrowth. As they came into the shadow of the church, she felt Hector's hand touch her waist. She gave a startled cry.

"How stupid!" she exclaimed as they came out of the shadow. "I thought I was being carried off by a ghost."

Hector laughed and offered his own explanation:

"It must have been the fennel brushing against your skirt."

They stopped to look at the crosses all around them and the profound stillness of the dead lying beneath their feet filled them with a strange tenderness. They moved on, full of suppressed emotion.

"You were scared; I heard you," said Monsieur Chabre. "It serves you right!"

At high tide, they would amuse themselves by going down to watch the arrival of the sardine boats; Hector would tell the Chabres when a sail was seen making for the harbour. But after seeing a few boats come in, Monsieur Chabre announced that it was always the same thing. Estelle on the other hand never seemed to weary of the scene and enjoyed going out onto the sea wall more and more. They often had to run. She would leap over the uneven stones, her skirts flying in the air, and she would catch hold of them to avoid tripping over. When she arrived, she was quite puffed and, putting her hand on her chest, she would throw her head back to regain her breath. With her dishevelled hair and devil-may-care boyish air, Hector found her adorable. Meanwhile the boat had tied up and the fishermen were carrying up their baskets of sardines which glistened in the sun like silver with blue and sapphire, pink and pale ruby-red tints. The young man always provided the same information: a basket contained a thousand sardines which would fetch a price fixed every morning according to the size of the catch; the fishermen would share the proceeds of the sale after handing over one third to the owner of the boat. Then the sardines would be salted straight away in wooden boxes with holes to allow the brine to drip away. However, Estelle and her companion gradually came to neglect the sardines. They would still go and see, but they didn't look. They would hurry down to the harbour and then return in silence, lazily gazing at the sea.

"Was it a good catch?" Monsieur Chabre would enquire each time they returned.

"Yes, very good," they would reply.

And every Sunday evening Piriac put on an open-air dance. The young men and girls of the district would join hands and dance round in a circle for hours on end, droning out the same strongly accentuated refrain, and as these harsh voices boomed out in the half-light, they gradually took on a kind of barbaric charm. As she sat on the beach with Hector lying at her feet, Estelle was soon sunk in daydreams. The sea came lapping in, gently but boldly; as it broke on the sand, it seemed like a voice full of passion suddenly stilled as the sound died away and the water receded with a plaintive murmur like a love that had now been tamed. And Estelle would sit dreaming of being loved by a giant whom she had succeeded in turning into a little boy.

"You must be bored in Piriac, my dear," Monsieur Chabre would occasionally say, in an enquiring tone, to his wife.

And she would hasten to reply:

"Oh no, not at all, I promise you."

She was, in fact, enjoying her stay in this remote, dead-and-alive little place. The geese and pigs and sardines had assumed great importance; even the little churchyard was a cheerful spot. This drowsy, unsociable sort of life in a village inhabited only by the grocer from Nantes and the deaf lawyer from Guérande seemed more exciting than the bustling existence of the fashionable resorts. After a fortnight, bored to tears, Monsieur Chabre would willingly have returned home to Paris. Surely the shellfish must have produced their effect by now, he said. But she protested:

"Oh no, my dear, you haven't had enough yet... I'm quite sure you need still more."

4

ONE EVENING, Hector said to the couple:
"Tomorrow there's an exceptionally low tide. We could go shrimping."

Estelle was delighted by the suggestion. Oh yes, they certainly must go and catch shrimps! She'd been looking forward to this excursion for ages! But Monsieur Chabre had objections. First of all, you never catch anything... Furthermore, it was much simpler to go and buy a franc's worth of shrimps from a local fisherman, without having to get wet up to your middle and scrape the skin off your feet. But in face of his wife's enthusiasm, he was forced to give way.

There were elaborate preparations. Hector undertook to provide the nets. Despite his dislike of cold water, Monsieur Chabre had expressed his willingness to participate and, once having agreed, he was determined to do the job properly. On the morning of the expedition, he had a pair of boots dubbined; he then dressed himself in white twill from top to toe, but his wife could not persuade him to forgo his bow tie, the ends of which he fluffed out as if he were going to a wedding. The bow tie was his protest, as a respectable member of society, against the slovenliness of the Atlantic. As for Estelle, she merely slipped a shift over her bathing costume. Hector was also wearing a bathing costume.

The three of them set off at about two o'clock in the afternoon with their nets over their shoulders. It was more than a mile across sand and seaweed to reach the rock where Hector had promised they would find plenty of shrimps. He piloted the couple towards their goal, taking them in a beeline through all the rock pools and calmly ignoring the hazards on the way. Estelle followed intrepidly, cheerfully paddling over the cool wet sand. Bringing up the rear, Monsieur Chabre could see no need to get his boots wet before they reached the shrimping grounds. He conscientiously skirted every pool, jumping over the channels of water left behind by the ebbing tide and cautiously picking his way over the dry spots like a true Parisian balancing himself on the tops of the paving sets on a muddy day in the Rue Vivienne. He was already out of breath and kept asking:

"Is it still a long way? Why can't we start shrimping here? I'm positive I can see some... Anyway, they're all over the place in the sea, aren't they? I bet you only need to push your net through the sand."

"Go ahead and push, Monsieur Chabre," replied Hector each time.

So in order to recover his breath, Monsieur Chabre would push his net along the bottom of a pool not much larger than a pocket handkerchief and as empty of shrimps as it was transparent. So he caught nothing, not even seaweed. Then he would set off again, pursing his lips and looking dignified, but as he lost ground each time he insisted on proving that there were shrimps everywhere, he ended by dropping a long way behind.

The tide was still going out, retreating almost a mile from the coast. As far as the eye could see, the rocky, pebbly sea bed was emptying out, leaving a vast, wet, uneven and desolate wilderness, like some storm-ravaged plain. In the distance the only visible thing was the green fringe of the still receding sea, as if being swallowed up by the land, while long, narrow bands of dark rock slowly emerged like promontories stretching out in the stagnant water. Estelle stopped to look at this immense, bare expanse.

"Isn't it big!" she murmured.

Hector pointed to a number of greenish rocks worn smooth by the waves.

"Those are only uncovered twice a month," he explained. "People go there to collect mussels. Can you see that brown spot over there? That's the Red Cow rocks, the best place to catch lobsters. You can't see them except at the two lowest tides of the year. But we must get a move on. We're going to those rocks over there whose tops are just beginning to show."

When they started to go into the sea, Estelle could hardly restrain her excitement. She kept lifting her feet high in the air and bringing them down with a splash, laughing as the spray shot up. Then, when the sea came up to her knees, she strode along, delighted to feel the water pressing hard against her thighs and surging between them.

"Don't be scared," said Hector, "You'll be getting into water up to your waist but it becomes shallower after that. We're nearly there."

And after crossing a narrow channel, they waded out of the water and climbed up on to a wide rocky platform uncovered by the tide. When the young woman looked round, she uttered a cry of surprise at seeing how far she had come from the shore. The houses of Piriac were just a line of tiny white spots stretching out along the shore, dominated by the square tower of its green-shuttered church. Never had she seen such a vast expanse, with the strip of sand gleaming in the bright sunlight and the dark green seaweed and brilliantly coloured rocks glistening with water. It was as if the earth had reached its uttermost limit in a heap of ruins on the brink of empty space.

Estelle and Hector were just about to start shrimping when they heard a plaintive call. It was Monsieur Chabre stuck in the middle of the channel and wanting to know which way to go. "How do I get across?" he was shouting. "Do I keep straight on?"

"Go to your left," called Hector.

He went to his left but the shock of finding himself in still deeper water again brought him to a halt. He did not dare even to retrace his steps.

"Come and help me," he wailed. "I'm sure there are holes round here. I can feel them…"

"Keep to your right, Monsieur Chabre, to your right!" shouted Hector.

And the poor man looked so funny in the middle of the water, with his net over his shoulder and his splendid bow tie, that Estelle and Hector could not refrain from sniggering. In the end he managed to find a way through but he arrived in a very nervous state and snapped angrily:

"I can't swim, you know."

He now began to worry about how to get back. When the young man explained to him how important it was not to be caught on the rock by the rising tide, he started becoming anxious again:

"You will warn me, won't you?"

"Don't worry, I'll look after you."

They all three started shrimping, probing the holes with their narrow nets. Estelle showed a feminine enthusiasm and it was she who caught the first shrimps, three large red ones which leapt about wildly in her net. She called out to Hector to help her because she was rather scared by their lively behaviour, but when she saw that they stopped moving as soon as you caught hold of them by their heads, she became bolder and had no trouble in slipping them herself into the little basket which she was carrying slung over her shoulder. Sometimes she netted a whole bunch of seaweed and had to rummage through it each time a sound like the fluttering of wings warned her that shrimps were hidden there. She sorted carefully through the seaweed, picking it up gingerly between finger and thumb, rather uneasy at the strange tangle of fronds, soft and slimy like dead fish. Now and again, she would peep impatiently into her basket, keen to fill it.

"How odd," Monsieur Chabre kept exclaiming. "I haven't caught a single one."

Being afraid of venturing between the gaps in the rocks and greatly hampered also by his boots which had become waterlogged, he was pushing his net along the sandy beach and thereby catching nothing but crabs, half a dozen or even up to ten of them at a time. They terrified him and he wrestled with his net to tip them out. Every so often he would turn anxiously round to see if the tide was still ebbing.

"You're sure it's still going out?" he kept asking.

Hector merely nodded; he was shrimping with all the assurance of a man who knows exactly where to go and as a result he was catching great handfuls of them with each sweep of his net. Whenever he found himself working beside Estelle, he would tip his catch into her basket while she kept laughing and giving a wink in the direction of her husband, with her finger to her lips. She looked most attractive as she bent forwards over the long wooden handle of her net or else leaning her blonde curly head over it as she eagerly peered to examine her catch. There was a breeze blowing and the water dripping from her net soaked her bathing costume with spray and made it cling to her, revealing every contour of her youthful body.

They had been shrimping like this for some two hours when she stopped for a rest, quite out of breath and with her honey-coloured curls damp with perspiration. The immense deserted seascape still spread out, peaceful and magnificent; only the sea could be seen shimmering in the distance, creating a murmur that seemed to be growing louder. The sun was blazing in a fiery sky; it was now four o'clock and its pale blue had turned almost grey, but this leaden, torrid heat was tempered and dispersed by the coolness of the water, and a gentle haze dimmed the harsh glare. Estelle was particularly charmed by the sight of a whole host of little black dots standing out very clearly on the horizon; they were shrimpers like themselves, incredibly delicate in outline and no larger than ants, ridiculous in their insignificance in the vast immensity; yet you could distinguish their every gesture, their shoulders hunched over their nets and their arms reaching out and gesticulating feverishly, like trapped flies, as they sorted out their catch, wrestling with the seaweed and the crabs.

"I assure you the tide's coming in," Monsieur Chabre called anxiously. "Look over there, that rock was uncovered a moment ago."

"Of course it's coming in," Hector retorted impatiently at last, "and that's exactly the time when you catch most shrimps."

But Monsieur Chabre was beginning to panic. At his last attempt he had just caught a strange fish, an anglerfish, whose freakish-looking head had terrified him. He had had enough.

"Come on, let's go. We must be going!" he kept repeating. "It's stupid to take risks."

"But we've just been telling you that it's the best time when the tide's starting to come in," his wife replied.

"And it's coming in with a vengeance!" Hector added in an undertone, with a mischievous glint in his eyes.

The waves were indeed beginning to roll in, booming as they swallowed up the rocks; a whole spit of sand would suddenly disappear, swamped by the sea. The breakers were triumphantly retaking possession of their age-old domain, foot by foot. Estelle had discovered a pool the bottom of which was covered in long fronds of seaweed, swirling round like strands of hair, and she was catching enormous shrimps, ploughing up long furrows with her net and leaving behind large swathes, like a reaper. She was thrashing around and determined not to be dragged away.

"All right then," Monsieur Chabre exclaimed in a tearful voice, "there's nothing to be done, I'm off. There's no sense in us all being cut off."

So he went off first, sounding the depth of the holes with the long handle of his shrimping net. When he had gone two or three hundred yards, Hector at last prevailed on Estelle to follow his example.

"We're going to be up to our shoulders," he said with a smile. "Monsieur Chabre's going to get a thorough wetting. Look how deep he is already."

Ever since the start of the outing, Hector had had the slightly furtive and preoccupied look of a young man in love and promising himself to declare his feelings, but he had not been able to pluck up courage to do so. As he had slipped his shrimps into Estelle's basket, he had indeed endeavoured to touch her fingers but it was plain that he was furious with himself for being so timorous. He would have been delighted to see Monsieur Chabre fall into a hole and drown, because, for the first time, he was finding the husband's presence a hindrance.

"I tell you what," he said suddenly, "you must climb up on my back and I'll give you a lift. Otherwise you're going to get soaked through. How about it? Up you get!"

He offered her his back but she blushed and declined, looking embarrassed. He, however, refused to take no for an answer, arguing that he was responsible for her safety. Eventually, she clambered up, placing her two hands on his shoulders. He stood as firm as a rock, straightened his back and set off, carrying her as lightly as a feather, telling her to hang on tight as he strode through the water.

"We've got to go right, haven't we?" Monsieur Chabre called out to Hector in a plaintive voice. The water was already up to his hips.

"That's it, keep going right," the young man called back.

Then, as the husband turned to go on, shivering with fright when he felt the water coming up to his armpits, Hector, greatly daring, kissed one of the tiny hands resting on his shoulder. Estelle tried to draw it away but Hector warned her to keep quite still or else he could not be responsible for what would happen. He started kissing her hand again: it was cool and salty and seemed to be offering all the bitter delights of the Ocean.

"Will you please stop doing that," Estelle kept protesting, trying to sound cross. "You're taking advantage of me. If you don't stop, I'll jump off."

He didn't stop, nor did she jump off. He was keeping a tight hold on her ankles while covering her hands with kisses, not saying a word but also keeping a close eye on Monsieur Chabre's back or at least all that could be seen of his pathetic back, now threatening to disappear beneath the waves at every step.

"Did you say keep to the right?" the husband called imploringly.

"Go left if you like!"

Monsieur Chabre took a step to his left and gave a cry. The water had come up to his neck, submerging his bow tie. Hector gratefully accepted the opportunity of making his declaration:

"I love you..."

"You're not to say that, I forbid it!"

"I love you... I adore you... I haven't had the courage to tell you so up till now because I was afraid of offending you."

He could not turn his head to look at her and continued to stride along with water up to his chest. Estelle could not refrain from laughing out loud at the absurdity of the situation.

"You must stop talking like that," she went on, adopting a motherly tone and giving him a slap on his shoulder. "Now, be a good boy and above all, mind you don't miss your step."

Feeling the slap on his shoulder, Hector was filled with joy: it was the seal of approval! And as poor Monsieur Chabre was still in trouble, Hector gave a cheerful shout:

"Keep straight on now!"

When they reached the beach, Monsieur Chabre attempted to give an explanation:

"'Pon my word, I was nearly caught. It's my boots," he stammered.

But Estelle opened her basket and showed him it, full of shrimps.

"Did you catch all those?" he exclaimed in amazement. "You certainly are a good shrimper!"

"Oh," she replied with a smile, "this gentleman showed me the way."

5

THE CHABRES HAD ONLY TWO DAYS LEFT IN PIRIAC. Hector seemed dismayed and furious, yet humble. As for Monsieur Chabre, he reviewed his health every morning and seemed puzzled.

"You can't possibly leave without visiting the Castelli rocks," Hector said one evening. "Let's organize an excursion for tomorrow."

He explained that the rocks were less than a mile away. They had been undermined by the waves and hollowed out into caves which extended for a mile and a half along the coast. According to him, they were completely unspoilt and wild.

"All right, we'll go tomorrow," said Estelle in the end. "Are they difficult to get at?"

"No, there are just a couple of spots where you have to wade through some shallow water, that's all."

But Monsieur Chabre did not want even to get his feet wet. Ever since his experience of almost going under during the shrimping expedition, he had harboured a grudge against the sea and so he expressed considerable opposition to Hector's suggestion. It was absurd to take risks like that: in the first place, he was not going to climb down to those rocks and risk breaking his leg jumping around like a goat; if he were absolutely compelled to, he would accompany them on the cliff path above and even that he would be doing only as a favour.

To make him relent, Hector had a sudden inspiration.

"I tell you what," he said, "you'll be going past the Castelli semaphore station. Well, you can call in there and buy some shellfish from the crew. They always have superb shellfish which they practically give away."

The ex-corn merchant perked up. "That's a good idea," he replied. "I'll take a little basket with me and I'll be able to have a final feast of shellfish."

And turning to his wife, he said with a leer: "Perhaps that'll do the trick."

Next day, they had to wait for low tide before they set off and, as Estelle was not ready in time, they in fact did not leave until five o'clock. However, Hector assured them that they would not be caught by the tide. The young woman was wearing cloth bootees over her bare feet and a very short and slightly raffish-looking grey linen dress which exposed a slim pair of ankles. As for Monsieur Chabre, he was dressed, most correctly, in a pair of white trousers and a long alpaca coat. He had brought his sunshade and a little basket; he had the appearance of a respectable middle-class Paris gentleman setting off on a shopping expedition.

Reaching the first of the rocks was awkward: they had to walk for some distance over quicksands in which their feet sank. The ex-corn merchant was soon puffing and blowing.

"All right then, I'll let you go on and I'll go up," he gasped at last.

"That's right, take that path there," Hector replied. "If you come any further, there's no way up. Would you like some help?"

They watched him climb to the top of the cliff. Once there, he opened his sunshade and, swinging his basket in the other hand, called down:

"I've done it, it's much better up here. Now, don't do anything rash, will you? Anyway, I'll be able to keep an eye on you from up here."

Hector and Estelle began walking over the rocks. The young man led the way, leaping from boulder to boulder in his high boots with the grace and agility of a mountaineer. Estelle followed intrepidly on the same stones and when he turned to ask:

"Shall I give you a hand?" she replied:

"Certainly not! Do you take me for a grandmother?"

They had now reached a vast floor of granite worn down by the sea and hollowed out into deep crevasses. It was like the skeleton of some sea monster whose dislocated vertebrae were protruding from the sand. In the hollows there was flowing water and dark seaweed was dangling like strands of hair. They continued to leap from stone to stone, pausing now and then to recover their balance and laughing each time they dislodged a boulder.

"They're rather tame, your rocks," said Estelle with a smile. "They wouldn't be out of place in a drawing room!"

"Just you wait," retorted Hector. "You'll see in a minute."

They had reached a narrow passage, a sort of gap between two enormous blocks of stone, and the way through was barred by a rock pool, a hole full of water.

"I'll never get across that!" the young woman exclaimed.

He suggested carrying her but she shook her head: she was not going to let herself be carried again. He then started looking round for some rocks big enough to make stepping stones, but they kept slipping and sinking to the bottom. Finally, losing patience, she said:

"Give me your hand, I'm going to jump."

She jumped short and one foot went into the water and this made them laugh again. Then, when they had gone through the passage, she stopped and exclaimed out loud in admiration.

In front of her lay a large round bay full of gigantic tumbled rocks, enormous blocks of stone standing like sentries keeping guard over the waves. All along the foot of the cliffs the land had been eroded by storms, leaving behind vast masses of bare granite, with creeks and promontories, unexpected inlets forming deep caverns and beaches littered with blackish slabs of marble looking like large stranded fish. It was like some Cyclopean town, battered and ravaged by the sea, with its battlements knocked down, its towers half demolished and its buildings toppled and lying in heaps of ruins. Hector showed Estelle every nook and cranny of these storm-wrecked ruins. She walked over sand as fine and yellow as gold dust, with pebbles speckled with mica glinting in the sun. She clambered over fallen rocks where she had, at times, to hang on with both hands to prevent herself from slipping into the crevasses. She went through natural porticos and triumphal archways curved like those in Romanesque churches or soaring pointed arches like those of Gothic cathedrals. She scrambled down into cool deserted hollows a good dozen yards square, charmed by the blue thistles and dark-green succulent plants standing out in contrast to the dark-grey walls of the rock face on which they grew, and delighted by the friendly little brown seabirds fluttering within her reach as they repeated their chirpy little calls. And what amazed her most was that, each time she turned round, she could see the ever-present blue line of the Atlantic stretching out, majestic and calm, between every block of rock.

"Ah, there you are!" cried Monsieur Chabre from the top of the cliff. "I was worried because I had lost sight of you... Aren't these heights terrifying?"

He was standing a good six yards back from the edge, shading himself under his parasol with his little basket hitched over his arm. He added:

"It's coming in fast, be careful!"

"There's plenty of time, never fear," replied Hector.

Meanwhile, Estelle had sat down and was gazing, speechless with admiration, at the vast horizon. In front of her three round pillars of granite, made smooth by the waves, were standing like the giant columns of a ruined temple. Behind them, bathed in the golden half-light of the evening, the open sea spread out, a royal blue speckled with gold. In the far distance she could see a brilliant white dot, a tiny sail skimming like a seagull over the surface of the water. The calm of evening was already reaching out over the pale blue sky. Never had she felt so overpowered by such an all-pervading tenderness and exquisitely voluptuous delight.

"Let's go," said Hector, gently touching her arm.

She gave a start and stood up, full of languor and acquiescence.

"That little house with the mast is the semaphore, isn't it?" called Monsieur Chabre. "I'm going to get some shellfish, I'll catch you up in a minute."

Then, in an attempt to shake off the listlessness that had overtaken her, Estelle set off running like a child, leaping over the puddles as she made towards the sea, seized by a sudden whim to climb to the top of a heap of rocks which would be completely surrounded by water at high tide. And when, after scrambling laboriously through the gaps in the rocks, she finally reached the top, she hoisted herself on to the highest point and was delighted to see that she could dominate the whole sweep of the tragically devastated coastline. She stood outlined in the pure sea air, her skirt fluttering like a flag in the breeze.

As she came down, she peered into every little crevice as she passed. In the smallest cranny, she could see tiny slumbering pools whose limpid surfaces were reflecting the sky like shining mirrors. On the bottom, emerald-green seaweed was growing, like some romantic forest. The only living creatures were large black crabs which leapt up like frogs before disappearing without even stirring up the water. The young woman had a dreamy look in her eyes as if she had been granted a glimpse into secret regions of a vast, mysterious and happy land.

When they had come back to the foot of the cliff, she noticed that her companion had filled his handkerchief with some limpets.

"They're for your husband," he said. "I'll take them up to him."

At that very moment, a disconsolate Monsieur Chabre came into sight.

"They hadn't even got a mussel at the semaphore," he shouted down to them. "You see, I was right not to want to come."

But on seeing Hector's limpets, he cheered up, and he was staggered at the young man's agility as he clambered up by a track known only to himself, over a cliff-face that seemed completely smooth rock. His descent was even more impressive.

"It's nothing, really," Hector said. "It's as easy as going upstairs once you know where the steps are."

Monsieur Chabre now suggested turning back: the sea was beginning to look threatening. So he begged his wife at least to find an easy way up to the top of the cliff. Hector laughed and replied that there was no way suitable for ladies; they would now have to go on to the end. In any case, they hadn't yet visited the caves. Monsieur Chabre was compelled to continue along the top of the cliffs by himself. As the sun was now much lower in the sky, he closed his parasol and used it as a walking stick. In his other hand, he held his basketful of limpets.

"Are you feeling tired?" Hector asked Estelle gently.

"A little bit," she replied and took hold of the arm which he offered. However, she was not tired, but her delicious feeling of languor was slowly spreading through her whole body and the emotion she had felt at seeing the young man hanging from the cliff-face had left her trembling inwardly. They were walking slowly over a beach composed of broken shells which crunched under their feet like a gravel garden path. Both had again fallen silent. He showed her two wide openings in the rock: the Monk's Hole and the Cat's Grotto. As they walked on over another beach of fine sand, they looked at each other, still without exchanging a word, and smiled. The tide was now coming in, rippling gently over the sand, but they did not hear it. Up above, Monsieur Chabre had started calling to them, but they did not hear him either.

"It's sheer madness!" the ex-corn merchant was shouting, waving his sunshade and swinging his basket of limpets. "Estelle! Monsieur

Hector! Listen to me! You're going to be cut off! Your feet are already getting wet."

But they did not feel the cool water lapping round their feet.

"What's the matter with him?" the young woman muttered at last.

"Oh, it's you, Monsieur Chabre," Hector called out. "There's no need to worry. We've only got the Lady's Cave to look at now."

Monsieur Chabre made a despairing gesture and repeated:

"It's sheer madness! You'll both be drowned."

They were no longer paying attention... To avoid the rising tide, they went along the foot of the cliff and finally came to the Lady's Cave. It was a grotto hollowed out of a vast block of granite that jutted out towards the sea. Its roof, extremely high and wide, was shaped like a dome. Storms had polished its walls until they shone like agate and the pink and blue veins in the dark rock formed magnificent patterns of arabesques like the barbaric handiwork of primitive artists decorating a grandiose bathroom for a sea goddess. The gravelly floor of the cave, still wet, was glittering like a bed of precious stones while at the far end there was a softer bed of dry yellow sand, so pale as to be almost white.

It was here that Estelle sat down to inspect the grotto.

"It's the sort of place you could live in," she murmured.

But now Hector at last seemed to become aware of the tide and his face assumed a look of dismay.

"Oh my goodness, we're caught! The sea's cut us off! We're going to have to wait for two hours..."

He went out and looked up at Monsieur Chabre who was standing on top of the cliff, just above the grotto. He told him that they were cut off.

"What did I tell you?" Monsieur Chabre cried triumphantly.

"But you refused to listen to me, didn't you? Is there any danger?"

"None at all," Hector replied. "The tide only comes fifteen or twenty feet into the cave. The only thing is that we shall have to wait a couple of hours before we can get out. There's nothing to be alarmed at."

Monsieur Chabre was annoyed: so they wouldn't be back by dinner time and he was already feeling hungry! It really was a mad sort of outing! Then he sat down, grumbling, on the short grass, placing his sunshade on his left and his basket of limpets on his right.

"Well, I'm going to have to wait, then," he called. "Go back to my wife and make sure she doesn't catch cold."

Back in the cave, Hector sat down beside Estelle. After a moment, silently, he ventured to reach out and take hold of her hand. She did not try to draw it away. She sat looking into the distance. Dusk was falling and the light of the dying sun was veiled by a gentle haze. On the horizon, the sky was taking on a tender tinge of deepest red and the sea grew slowly darker, stretching out with not a soul in sight. The tide crept gently into the cave, quietly lapping over the glittering shingle and murmuring a promise of exquisite sea pleasures with its disturbing salty tang of desire.

"I love you, Estelle," Hector said, smothering her hands in kisses.

Choking with emotion, she made no reply, as though uplifted on the rising tide. She was by now half-lying on the bed of fine sand, looking like some sea nymph, caught unawares and already at his mercy.

Monsieur Chabre's voice abruptly broke in, faint and hollow:

"Aren't you hungry? I'm ravenous! Fortunately I've got my penknife, so I'll have a first instalment of my limpets."

"I love you, Estelle," said Hector again, taking her in his arms.

The night was dark and the pale sea lit up the sky. At the mouth of the grotto, a plaintive murmur was rising from the water while a last gleam of light deserted the top of the domed roof. The sea rippled and a scent of fruitfulness was hanging in the air. Slowly Estelle's head sank on to Hector's shoulder and on the evening air the breeze carried away a murmur of sighs.

Up above, by the light of the stars, Monsieur Chabre was methodically chewing away at his limpets and giving himself indigestion as he ate the whole lot, without any bread.

6

NINE MONTHS AFTER HER RETURN TO PARIS, the lovely Madame Chabre gave birth to a bouncing boy. A delighted Monsieur Chabre took Dr Guiraud aside and said proudly:

"It was the limpets that did the trick, I'm absolutely convinced of it! I ate a whole basketful of them one evening, in very peculiar circumstances, by the way. Anyway, never mind the details, doctor, but I never thought shellfish could have such remarkable effects."

Note on the Texts

Publication details and original titles of each story can be found in the following Notes. For editions of the stories in French, please see the Select Bibliography on p. 136.

Notes

p. 3, CAPTAIN BURLE (*Le Capitaine Burle*): The last of Zola's stories for *Vestnik Evropy*, it appeared in Russia in December 1880. It was published twice separately in French periodicals before giving its title to a collection of six short stories from *Vestnik Evropy* published in a single volume in 1882; they included 'The Way People Die' (*Comment on meurt*, which can be found in *Attack on the Mill and Other Stories*, published by Alma Classics) and 'Coqueville on the Spree' (*La Fête à Coqueville*). A further volume of six *Vestnik Evropy* stories followed in 1884; it took its title from *Naïs Micoulin* ('A Flash in the Pan', also in *Attack on the Mill and Other Stories*), and included 'Dead Men Tell No Tales' *(La Mort d'Olivier Bécaille)*, 'Shellfish for Monsieur Chabre' (*Les Coquillages de Monsieur Chabre*) and 'Absence Makes the Heart Grow Fonder' *(Jacques Damour*, also in *Attack on the Mill and Other Stories)*.

   If 'Captain Burle' is possibly the most squalid of all Zola's short stories, it is perhaps also, through its paucity of light relief, one of his most disturbing. There is little comfort for optimists in this tale of family pride leading a mother to instigate her son's death and drive her grandson to an early grave, and of military honour bringing about the death of an officer at the hands of an old friend.

p. 4, *Solferino*: An Italian village in the province of Mantua, the scene of a victory of Napoleon III's army over the Austrians in June 1859.

p. 9, *absinthe*: A wormwood-flavoured French rotgut liqueur; its sale was later banned.

p. 35, COQUEVILLE ON THE SPREE *(La Fête à Coqueville)*: Published in *Vestnik Evropy* in August 1879, in French in May 1880. This story shows flashes of optimism of a sort rare in Zola: it seems to be suggested that man's natural goodness, here released by massive doses of free alcohol, can rise above influences of history and environment. But Zola obviously has tongue in cheek, and the only glimpse into the future shows the downtrodden Monsieur Mouchel tanning the hide off the acerbic Madame Veuve Dufeu.

p. 35, *Louis XIII*: Takes us back to the period 1610–43.

p. 37, *Brisemotte*: French for a "clod-crusher", a sort of harrow – but an earlier familiar meaning of *motte* was the mons Veneris.

p. 37, *La Queue... Louis Philippe... pigtail*: Louis Philippe reigned from 1830–48, long after pigtails (French, *queue*) were outmoded.

p. 39, *the Emperor*: Strange to have been so called because he had served under a king, but nicknames are like that, and anything imperial is military. Charles X reigned from 1824 to 1830.

p. 39, *sous-préfet*: For administrative purposes, France is divided into ninety-odd *départements*, each under a *préfet*, and each *département* is subdivided into *arrondissements* of which the head is a *sous-préfet*.

p. 48, *ratafia*: A liqueur flavoured with almond, peach, apricot or cherry kernels.

p. 55, *tuica calugaresca... Serbian slivovitz*: Zola obviously enjoyed dredging up the names of very exotic spirits and liqueurs: even in our well-travelled, affluent age, while Serbian (or Yugoslavian) slivovitz is not unfamiliar to many, Romanian tuica calugareasca (misspelt by Zola) – also a plum brandy – is less likely to be widely known. "Calugareasca" tells us that, like trappistine (made by Trappist monks), this tuica is made by monks.

p. 63, DEAD MEN TELL NO TALES *(La Mort d'Olivier Bécaille)*: Published in *Vestnik Evropy* in March 1879 and in France a month later (see note to 'Captain Burle' above). The story reveals an underlying morbidity in Zola.

p. 63, *Rue Dauphine*: In the sixth arrondissement, on the Left Bank near Saint-Germain-des-Prés.

p. 85, *my sense of direction*: Bécaille must have been buried in the Montparnasse cemetery, like the Comte de Verteuil in 'The Way People Die'.

p. 89, SHELLFISH FOR MONSIEUR CHABRE *(Les Coquillages de Monsieur Chabre)*: Published in *Vestnik Evropy* in September 1876; section four appeared separately in France in July 1881, and the whole story appeared in the collection of stories published under the general title of *Naïs Micoulin* in 1884 (see note to 'Captain Burle' above).

Zola wrote that the chief character in this story was the sea (he had holidayed in Piriac, on the Atlantic coast south of Nantes, in 1876, and many personal memories of the landscape have been incorporated). It is also an excellent manual of seduction for the use of males and females.

Extra Material

on

Émile Zola's

Dead Men Tell No Tales
and Other Stories

Émile Zola's Life

Émile Zola was born in Paris on 2nd April 1840, the son of Birth and Childhood Francesco Zolla, an Italian civil engineer from Venice, and Émilie Aubert, from a small town near Chartres. Zola spent his early life in Aix-en-Provence. His father, in charge of the construction of a canal to supply Aix with drinking water, died in 1847, and the Canal Zola was only completed in 1854. The young Émile was deeply affected by the death of his father, which seems to have resulted in an increased sense of attachment to his mother. She faced great difficulties raising him on her own, although she did have the support of her parents, who had also moved to Aix two years previously. The Zola household was now quite impoverished, which led Émilie in 1849 to embark on an ultimately fruitless decade of legal wranglings with the Société du Canal Zola in order to keep the modest pension they paid her and receive due compensation for her shares.

Despite this loss, Zola's childhood appears to have been an Youth idyllic and happy one. His mother allowed him much freedom, although she was also very protective of her young son, who was small and sickly and stuck out in southern France with his Parisian accent. But by the time Émile was eight, it became clear to her that he needed schooling, which was beyond her means at the time. After a term spent at the Pension Notre-Dame, Émile was enrolled on a scholarship at the Collège Bourbon, a Jesuit school where Aix notables and rich farmers sent their children. On the one hand, the Collège Bourbon was austere to the point of extreme discomfort, renowned for terrible food and the absence of heating, but on the other it was remarkably lax compared to most Jesuit establishments and offered beautiful premises. Zola was one of the top students during his six years there, when he won prizes in French narration – he later claimed he was spurred on by the shadow of his father and the fact that he knew he would later in life be dependent on his own efforts – but he was also fond of camaraderie and the countryside. Despite initially suffering the harassment reserved for beneficiaries of bursaries, he made long-standing friends there, the most famous of them being the future Impressionist painter Paul Cézanne. During this period, he read widely, especially authors such as Dumas, Sue, Féval, Hugo, Lamartine and Musset.

Move to Paris   When her mother Henriette died and things came to a head in her legal action, requiring her to be in Paris, Mme Zola moved to the capital at the end of 1857, with Émile and his grandfather joining her in February of the following year. Through a connection, his mother managed to secure a place for him at the prestigious Lycée Saint-Louis, where the shy, provincial and impecunious eighteen-year-old Zola again found it difficult to fit in. He missed Aix-en-Provence and his friends there, and found it difficult to keep up academically in Paris, although he did win the second prize for narration. That autumn he fell gravely ill for several months, and failed his *baccalauréat* in science twice in 1859.

Hardship   This scuppered his plan to become an engineer and, in 1860, faced with the increasing impoverishment he and his mother were experiencing, he briefly took on a clerk's position at the customs house of the Canal Saint-Martin. The drudgery of this occupation made him miserable. In 1862, after various office jobs and periods of unemployment – which did however enable him to read extensively and start moving in artistic circles – Zola began work, thanks to a family friend, with Hachette and Company, France's most important publishing house. Initially placed in the post room, he was soon promoted by his employers to the publicity department, where he eventually became the manager. Working in this department provided him with the platform to launch a literary career, as it enabled him to learn how the milieu operated and meet many established authors on Hachette's books, as well as journalists and new talent. He began to write short stories: 1863 saw the publication of two of them, which appeared with several more in the collection published in November 1864, *Stories for Ninon*. In 1865 appeared *The Confession of Claude*, an autobiographical novel written in the first person, recounting a young man's (illicit) initiation into the ways of love. At this early stage, a key feature of Zola's career was already in evidence, namely the parallel output in the fields of literature and journalism: Zola had regular articles and columns in the press, and in 1866 was able to leave Hachette to take up a position as columnist with *L'Événement*. It is worth stressing that Zola – though clearly a highly original, distinctive and extraordinarily prolific writer – is somewhat symptomatic of a phenomenon which, though by no means unprecedented, became the norm over the course of the nineteenth century as publishing and the press became mass industries, and culture as well as society became increasingly democratized. This was the phenomenon of the professional author who lived from writing, as opposed to the gentleman of leisure, whose private income allowed time for literary pursuits. The dual character of Zola's early activities also foreshadows another distinctive aspect of his career: the involvement of the writer in the domain of public affairs. As for his private life, he began a relationship with Alexandrine Meley, who would become his wife in 1870.

After the publication in 1867 of his successful but con- *The Rougon-Macquart* troversial novel *Thérèse Raquin*, Zola sent a plan to its *Series* publisher Albert Lacroix for a series of ten novels – which was to become known as the *Rougon-Macquart* cycle – about various members and generations of a family living during the social transformations and political upheavals of the previous two decades. This was not an altogether unusual project for a politically engaged journalist contributing to a number of opposition newspapers on matters of political actuality. Nor was Zola, on the literary front, necessarily doing anything particularly original per se in writing a series of novels about contemporary French society: this type of totalizing social vision had also been expressed some decades previously in Balzac's *Human Comedy*, a cycle of novels containing numerous recurring characters and depicting the panoply of human activity in Restoration France. Zola himself had written a series of interlinked stories about urban life, *The Mysteries of Marseille* (1867), its title alluding to Eugène Sue's melodramatic serial work *The Mysteries of Paris* (1842–43).

What was strikingly original about Zola's planned series was that it combined this preoccupation with depicting the totality of the modern world with what he referred to in the plan sent to Lacroix as "questions of blood and milieux". That is, there was to be an underlying theme founded on the rapidly developing science of heredity, the key aspect of a broadly deterministic scientific basis for the motivation of fictional characters living in various modern environments. Zola's stated intention was to "rummage around in the very heart of the human drama, in those depths of life where great virtues and great crimes come into being, and to rummage there in a methodical fashion, led by the guiding thread of new physiological discoveries". This would facilitate the other broad aim, namely "to study the Second Empire, from the *Coup d'État* to the present day". In 1869, Zola finished the first novel in the series, *The Fortune of the Rougons*, charting the origins of his fictional family and its involvement in major political upheavals, and Lacroix offered him a contract for the whole series, which developed from the originally planned ten-volume work into a cycle of twenty novels published as separate volumes – usually after their appearance in serial form – between 1871 and 1893.

Height of Success   In 1870, in the middle of the Franco-Prussian conflict, Zola worked for the war-time government in Bordeaux. After another brief spell away from the capital during the bloody Paris Commune episode the following spring, Zola began enjoying unprecedented success as a novelist and public figure. He published novels in his *Rougon-Macquart* series at the rate of almost one a year. As well as the various artists he had been associating himself with and whom he often defended in his articles, he established friendships with many of the most important authors of the time, such as Flaubert, Daudet, Maupassant, Turgenev and Mallarmé. The seventh *Rougon-Macquart* novel, *L'Assommoir*, was a commercial and critical sensation, although – like most of his novels – it polarized readers and reviewers, with some left shocked by its graphic depictions of poverty and alcoholism. The sales of that book meant that he was able to afford a villa in Médan in 1878, to which he had several extensions made in subsequent years. In 1881 he was elected as a local councillor to the town of Médan, and on 14th July 1888 he was awarded the French Legion of Honour. To his great annoyance, however, he failed in successive bids, from 1889 onwards, to be voted into the prestigious Académie Française.

This successful period had its difficult moments, such as the death in October 1880 of his beloved mother, which came shortly after the passing away of Flaubert, who had become a kind of father figure as well as a friend. He was also periodically beset by ill health, suffering mostly from complaints of a nervous nature.

During this period, there was a major twist in his domestic *Jeanne Rozerot* situation: much like the protagonist in the final *Rougon-Macquart* novel, *Doctor Pascal* – the story of the ageing documenter of the Rougon-Macquart family rejuvenating himself in the arms of a young woman – Zola found a new love in his life. He had been married to Alexandrine Meley since 1870, and indeed remained with her for the rest of his life, but in 1888 he began a long-term affair with Jeanne Rozerot, a twenty-one-year-old Burgundian who had entered into service in the Zola household. Very soon Zola had installed her in an apartment in Paris, to which he would make frequent visits, and in 1889 she gave birth to a daughter, Denise, followed by a son, Jacques, in 1891. After Alexandrine discovered the affair in 1892 thanks to an anonymous letter, there was a mutually accepted arrangement, whereby Jeanne and the children lived as part of the Zola family.

It has been written that this new-found romantic and family bliss, although fulfilling Zola the man, somewhat took the edge off Zola the author – indeed his subsequent novel cycle, *The Three Cities*, failed to capture the public's imagination in the same way his previous series did, and has received less acclaim – perhaps somewhat unfairly – to this day. Zola also felt that he was the subject of unjust criticism, as he was sometimes portrayed as being insensitive, hard-hearted and excessively motivated by financial gain. Partly, perhaps, in order to dispel this image, he consented to be the first subject of Dr Édouard Toulouse's "medico-psychological" study, which aimed to investigate the pathologies of intellectually gifted individuals. Toulouse concluded that Zola was mentally stable and well balanced, and the author himself claimed in the preface to the published report that he had always been spurred on by the pursuit of truth above everything else.

Zola soon had a chance to demonstrate his commitment to *The Public Intellectual:* truth and justice. No event illustrates better the engagement *the Dreyfus Affair* of the writer in public life than the Dreyfus affair, which created, or rather perhaps exacerbated, a political chasm in

French society during the 1890s and still has repercussions today. Captain Alfred Dreyfus, a Jewish army officer, was falsely accused of passing French military secrets to Germany, and in 1894 was found guilty, forced to undergo a military degradation ceremony and sentenced to life imprisonment on the penal colony of Devil's Island.

After the acquittal at the beginning of 1898 of Commandant Ferdinand Walsin Esterhazy, for whose involvement in the initial passing of information there had been compelling evidence (pointing by implication to Dreyfus's innocence), an open letter from Zola to Félix Faure, President of the Republic, which has come to be known – after its banner headline – as 'J'Accuse!', was published in the newspaper *L'Aurore* on 13th January. In the letter, in fact quite a lengthy article, Zola took to pieces the case against Dreyfus and catalogued the deceit of individuals within the military high command in doing their best to keep an innocent man in prison, exile and ignominy, for the sake of shoring up the authority of the army and the state. The following month Zola was tried for having accused the court-martial of knowingly acquitting a guilty man, and sentenced to a year in prison. The conviction was quashed on appeal, but a further writ emerged, and in July 1898 Zola fled to England for a year – during which time he was stripped of his Legion of Honour – remaining in exile until, in June 1899, a review of the case was ordered, vindicating Zola and allowing him to return. The sequence of events arising from 'J'Accuse!' meant that the details of the case were aired fully, and a retrial was ordered: Dreyfus's sentence was cut down to ten years' hard labour in 1899, and he was subsequently pardoned and released.

The End   After the Dreyfus affair, Zola's stamina was undiminished, and he launched himself into his next project, a four-volume series entitled *The Four Gospels*. He managed to complete the first three, *Fecundity*, *Work* and *Truth*, but the fourth volume of this Utopian cycle, to be entitled *Justice*, never materialized. Zola died on 29th September 1902 of asphyxiation, after inhaling carbon monoxide fumes from a blocked fireplace in his Paris apartment. The circumstances of Zola's death were suspicious, and there has been speculation ever since that he may have been poisoned. Zola certainly had many enemies, not least over his role in the Dreyfus affair, which had still not been brought to its definitive conclusion, so such conjecture cannot be dismissed lightly as conspiracy theory. Whatever its cause, precisely because of the controversy it continues to arouse, Zola's death is further testimony to the power and significance of the figure of the writer in the public domain. Buried initially in Montmartre cemetery, Zola's remains were removed to the Panthéon in 1908 – a clear and unambiguous acknowledgement of his contribution to French national life.

Émile Zola's Works

Since Zola was a professional writer and journalist, the extent of his writings is vast to say the least. From an early age, he composed poetry, and later in his career he made attempts to write for the theatre as well. He was also a prolific letter-writer throughout his life. By necessity, this section focuses on Zola's major works of fiction, but it should be borne in mind that these form part of a much larger body of work.

Zola's work from the late 1860s onwards begins to engage not only with history, politics and the modernity of a society undergoing rapid urbanization and industrialization, but also with philosophical, sociological, medical and technological ideas and developments. And present from the outset is a spirit of specifically scientific, empirically observational enquiry, which later comes to play a significant role in the literary movement associated with Zola, known as Naturalism.

Thérèse Raquin and Naturalism

Although Naturalism did not immediately declare itself as such and was not comprehensively formulated until many years later, one of the movement's key features, that of a certain kind of scientific determinism, is already to be found in Zola's 1867 novel, *Thérèse Raquin*, in which the title character and her sweetheart kill her husband (who is also her cousin) in order to be together, only to find that their horror and guilt over their action prevents them from enjoying their life together as lovers. The initial action prompts a logical development: a psychological decline in both characters which leads to the seemingly inevitable conclusion of insanity and suicide, which are presented not as supernaturally ordained moral just deserts, but as *naturally* determined consequences as physiological as they are psychological. *Thérèse Raquin* is in some sense a prototype for the Naturalist novel, though there are others, such as Zola's next book, *Madeleine Férat*,

131

the Goncourt brothers' *Germinie Lacerteux* or – as Zola would later claim himself – Flaubert's *Sentimental Education*. However, *Thérèse Raquin* and *Madeleine Férat* are rather one-dimensional works. It is Zola's next project which develops Naturalism's remarkably wide-ranging scope as a form of literature which deals with all aspects of modern life and is underpinned by modern ideas from varied fields.

The Rougon-Macquart Cycle *The Rougon-Macquarts*, subtitled *Natural and Social History of a Family under the Second Empire*, is the story of two branches, one legitimate (Rougon), the other illegitimate (Macquart), of a family from Plassans, a town in the South of France usually held to be a fictionalized version of Aix-en-Provence. However, it is also the story – or indeed set of stories – of the wider context of the period in which it is set, namely the Second Empire, the authoritarian regime of Louis-Napoléon Bonaparte, Napoleon III, which styled itself on the Empire of his uncle, Napoleon I. The Second Empire began with Bonaparte's *coup d'état* against the faltering Second Republic on 2nd December 1851, and ended in his ignominious defeat by Prussia at Sedan in September 1870, ushering in the Third Republic. The period was a time of great social and political change, most notably in infrastructural and economic terms. Under the direction of Baron Eugène-Charles Haussmann, Prefect of the Seine, Paris was transformed from a labyrinth of narrow medieval streets to an efficient network of boulevards facilitating circulation between all parts of the city and rapid movement to the new railway terminals and beyond; through state support the railways expanded massively, especially after 1860, to the extent that by 1870 all major cities were within twenty-four hours of Paris, and passenger numbers had increased within twenty-five years from 6 to 100 million. The economy – not least because of the developments in Paris – shifted to a model based on property speculation and capital investment in industry.

During this period, characterized by unprecedented capitalist growth subordinated to massive state intervention and control, France, though still at this stage a rural nation over much of its territory, acquired all the characteristics of a modern industrialized country. And it is France's adjustment to urban modernity, industry and capitalism that represents a significant element of Zola's novelistic project. As well as charting the political birth pangs and death throes of the period, the *Rougon-Macquart* cycle depicts – in a highly systematic way – modern social and industrial trends and institutions, as the following examples illustrate.

The second novel in the series, *The Kill* (1871), examines the mad rush for property in the new Paris being constructed by Haussmann. *The Belly of Paris* (1873) shows in intimate detail the workings of the central food markets in Paris, and exploits the metaphorical potential of the idea of digestion, showing economic competition as a struggle between fat and lean (a theme taken up elsewhere in the series, notably in *Germinal*). *L'Assommoir* (1876) provides a tragic account of alcoholism among the urban poor in a transforming city, which was a major breakthrough in making Zola a household name. His reputation for crude realism was enhanced by the publication of *Nana* (1880), a novel about the oldest profession in its most up-to-date Parisian context, in which the eponymous anti-heroine's prostitution – seen as poisoning the entire social body during the build-up to war and the collapse of the regime – is attributed to her forebears' drunkenness. The modern workplace is also a major theme: *Ladies' Delight* (1883) is a story set in one of the new Parisian department stores selling mass-produced consumer goods, while *Germinal* (1885) deals with industrial unrest in a mining community in northern France. *The Masterpiece* (1886), over which Cézanne – on whom the central character Claude Lantier was allegedly based – fell out with Zola, is a novel about the world of art (and its relationship with writing) in an age when, at last, modern representational techniques could represent modern life. Another recurrent feature in Zola's work is that of the network: *The Human Beast* (1890) is a crime novel centred on the railway, represented as a body spreading its interconnected tentacles throughout the national territory; *Money* (1891) represents the world of high finance as a circulatory system (as indeed does Karl Marx – regularly alluded to in the novel – in *Capital*). These two novels also have in common a sense of impending catastrophe, metaphorically figuring the collapse of the Second Empire, a collapse given concrete and literal expression in *The Debacle* (1892), a novel about Jean Macquart's experience in the Franco-Prussian war. Although each of the novels just cited has its own specific focus, they are all, in their representation of the workings of various systems (social, bodily, technological, institutional, economic), in some way about the mechanisms of society as a whole: not only do they illustrate how the system functions, they also typically show what happens when it falls into dysfunction – a dysfunction implicitly presented as being inherent in the system rather than brought about through external intervention. So, on the one hand, there is a totalizing depiction of the society of the middle of the nineteenth century (and in some sense also of that of the Third Republic, during which Zola wrote most of the novels); on the other hand, this is intimately connected with the "family" aspect of Zola's fictional cycle, itself informed by the novelist's engagement with new developments in science, medicine and technology.

As the cycle developed, the main features of Naturalism began to cohere: extreme and profuse detail, scientific determinism, the hereditary underpinning, the incorporation of knowledge from various fields and engagement with the modern world. Two elements in particular are worth bearing in mind. Firstly, documentary exactitude based on research and empirical observation. Naturalism is sometimes – with some justification – portrayed as an extreme offshoot of earlier Realism, in its concern for accuracy and its refusal to spare any information, no matter how gruesome or shocking. But it is perhaps in the area of documentary precision and the research necessary for it that Zola's Naturalism most impressively fulfils the Realist brief to represent the modern world as it is. While preparing *Germinal*, for example, Zola went down a mine in northern France, and observed the labour and living conditions of the miners and their families; for *The Human Beast*, he arranged to travel on the footplate of a locomotive, engaged in lengthy correspondence with railway employees and read several technical works on the railways. And *Ladies' Delight* presents a detailed analysis of the various mechanisms involved in the functioning of the modern department store; the store in the novel is based on two Parisian department stores – Le Bon Marché, which still exists, and Le Louvre – where Zola carried out research, involving interviews with staff. No stone was left unturned in the mission to represent reality accurately, and in accordance with "natural" (rather than metaphysical or idealistic) principles.

Naturalism, however, was not as coherent a system as Zola's rhetoric – deployed in *The Experimental Novel*, *Naturalism in the Theatre* (1881) and elsewhere – might have liked to claim, and a number of Naturalist features were more prominent in some novels than in others. If we consider *Germinal*, for instance, the stress is on the heredity theme, expressed by generations of miners inheriting obeisance and resignation to a miserable life, and the fantastical "machine-monster" metaphor of the mine as a devouring ogre. In *The Human Beast*, we have perhaps the closest thing to "total" Naturalism, in which the character of a psychopathic engine driver whose uncontrollable urge to kill, inherited – like his sister Nana's tendency to prostitution – from his alcoholic forebears, is paralleled in the relentless, unstoppable, mathematical inexorability of his locomotive's functioning. Other novels are Naturalist in the sense that they deal with the natural cycles of the earth, in particular *The Joy of Life* (1884) and *Earth* (1887), which both have rural settings. Others are concerned explicitly with the family history – such as *The Fortune of the Rougons*, *The Conquest of Plassans* (1874) and *Doctor Pascal* (1893). Others have a more institutional emphasis, focusing on politics – such as *His Excellency Eugène Rougon* (1876), in which the hero scales the commanding heights of the Bonapartist regime – or religion, such as *Abbé Mouret's Transgression* (1875), addressing the problematic question of celibacy, and *The Dream* (1888), set around an ancient cathedral.

Doctor Pascal (1893) brings to an end the *Rougon-Macquart* cycle in a highly self-referential way: Pascal Rougon drafts the family tree from a series of dossiers which he has built up on his relatives from both sides of the extended family. The final version of the family tree is presented with the last novel, which updates the versions provided with *The Fortune of the Rougons*. The cycle ends with the death of Pascal and simultaneously the birth of his child with his niece Clotilde, identified only as "the unknown child" on the family tree. This child is symbolic of the ultimate optimism of the *Rougon-Macquart* series, which does nevertheless have some very gloomy moments.

Zola's later novels continue in the life-affirmingly opti- *The Three Cities* mistic, quasi-religious vein of *Doctor Pascal*, the final instalment of the *Rougon-Macquart* series. His next project was a trilogy, *The Three Cities*, consisting of *Lourdes* (1894), *Rome* (1896) and *Paris* (1897). Inspired initially by a visit to Lourdes – which, after Bernadette Soubirous claimed to have seen the Virgin Mary there in 1858, had become a major pilgrimage centre and rallying point for religious fervour in the face of an emboldened rationalism – the trilogy deals with questions of faith, doubt and reason in the modern age. Its central character, a priest called Pierre Froment, has a crisis of faith and at the same time warms to a progressive Catholic socialism, on which grounds he is summoned to Rome to account for himself. Froment's development might be seen in the light of a sea change in the Vatican under the pontificate of Leo XIII, under whom the Church began to accommodate itself with modernity in a way unimaginable under his ultraconservative predecessor Pius IX. Ultimately, Pierre loses his faith, is defrocked and finds redemption in work, love and the fight for social justice.

The Four Gospels   As with the earlier trilogy, the *Four Gospels* cycle raises the possibility of a secularized replacement for Christianity in an age of reason and progress. *Fecundity* (1899), as its title suggests, celebrates the remarkable extent of the progeny of Pierre Froment's son and his wife Marianne, and articulates the potential for French civilization to spread itself throughout a fertile and receptive world. *Work* (1901) depicts a religion of humanity trumping both Christianity and capitalism in an ideal worker-owned neo-Fourierist workplace which Luc Froment has created from an abominable steelworks. *Truth* (published posthumously in 1903) relates the Dreyfus Affair in disguise, in a small-town setting. As we have seen above, the fourth volume of the series, *Justice*, was never completed.

– Larry Duffy, 2008

Select Bibliography

Many of the original manuscripts of the short stories have been lost (see 'Les "Manuscrits perdus" d'Émile Zola' in *Les Cahiers naturalistes*, no. 39, 1970, pp. 84–6). Printed texts of the stories, either in their various versions in periodicals or in volume form are available in the Bibliothèque Nationale in Paris and, in part, in the British Library in London.

Three of the main twentieth-century editions of the short stories are: *Contes et nouvelles*, ed. Maurice le Blond 2 vols. (Paris: Bernouard, 1928); *Contes et nouvelles*, ed. Henri Mitterand, vol. 9 of *Œuvres complètes* (Paris: Cercle du Livre

Précieux, 1970); *Émile Zola, Contes et nouvelles*, ed. Roger Ripoll (Paris: Gallimard, Bibliothèque de la Pléiade, 1976).

Biographies:
Brown, Frederick, *Zola. A Life* (London: Macmillan, 1995)
Hemmings, F.W.J., *Émile Zola* (Oxford: Clarendon Press, 1965)
Mitterand, Henri, *Zola*, 3 vols. (Paris: Fayard, 1999–2002)
Richardson, Joanna, *Zola* (London: Weidenfeld & Nicolson, 1978)
Wilson, Angus, *Émile Zola: An Introductory Study of His Novels* (London: Secker and Warburg, 1952)

Additional Recommended Reading:
Baguley, David, 'Maupassant avant la lettre? A study of a Zola short story, 'Les Coquillages de M. Chabre'', *Nottingham French Studies*, 6 (October 1967), pp. 77–86
Nelson, Brian, ed., *The Cambridge Companion to Zola* (Cambridge: Cambridge University Press, 2007)
Ricatte, Robert, 'Zola conteur', *Europe* (April–May 1968), pp. 209–17
Triomphe, Jean, 'Zola collaborateur du 'Messager d'Europe'', *Revue de Littérature Comparée*, 17, no. 4 (1937), pp. 754–65

On the Web:
abu.cnam.fr/BIB/auteurs/zolae.html
gallica.bnf.fr/classique
www.chass.utoronto.ca/french/sable/collections/zola/

ALMA CLASSICS

ALMA CLASSICS aims to publish mainstream and lesser-known European classics in an innovative and striking way, while employing the highest editorial and production standards. By way of a unique approach the range offers much more, both visually and textually, than readers have come to expect from contemporary classics publishing.

LATEST TITLES PUBLISHED BY ALMA CLASSICS

www.almaclassics.com